Drug Lords

Ghost

Lock Down Publications and Ca$h
Presents

Drug Lords

A Novel by *Ghost*

Ghost

Lock Down Publications
P.O. Box 870494
Mesquite, Tx 75187

Visit our website @
www.lockdownpublications.com

Copyright 2019 by Ghost
Drug Lords

Lock Down Publications
Like our page on Facebook: Lock Down Publications @
www.facebook.com/lockdownpublications.ldp
Cover design and layout by: **Dynasty Cover Me**
Book interior design by: **Shawn Walker**
Edited by: **Sunny Giovanni**

4

Stay Connected with Us!

Text **LOCKDOWN** to 22828 to stay up-to-date with new releases, sneak peaks, contests and more…

Thank you.

Submission Guideline.

Submit the first three chapters of your completed manuscript to ldpsubmissions@gmail.com, subject line: Your book's title. The manuscript must be in a .doc file and sent as an attachment. Document should be in Times New Roman, double spaced and in size 12 font. Also, provide your synopsis and full contact information. If sending multiple submissions, they must each be in a separate email.

Have a story but no way to send it electronically? You can still submit to LDP/Ca$h Presents. Send in the first three chapters, written or typed, of your completed manuscript to:

LDP: Submissions Dept
Po Box 870494
Mesquite, Tx 75187

DO NOT send original manuscript. Must be a duplicate.

Provide your synopsis and a cover letter containing your full contact information.

Only if your submission is **approved**, will you then get a response letter.

Thanks for considering LDP and Ca$h Presents.

Dedications:

First of all, this book is dedicated to my Baby Girl 3/10, the love of my life and purpose for everything I do. As long as I'm alive, you'll never want nor NEED for anything. We done went from flipping birds to flipping books. The best is yet to come.

To LDP'S CEO- Ca$h & COO- Shawn:

I would like to thank y'all for this opportunity. The wisdom, motivation, and encouragement that I've received from you two is greatly appreciated.

The grind is real. The loyalty in this family is real. I'm riding with LDP 'til the wheels fall off.

THE GAME IS OURS!

Ghost

Chapter 1

White snow fell from the sky in thick patches. The harsh wind caused the flakes to swirl about as if they were seconds away from turning into a collective blizzard. The temperature had dropped ten degrees below zero.

Makaroni pulled his hood firmer over his head. He stood at five feet ten inches tall with a Hershey dark chocolate complexion, sporting a low cut with deep, natural waves. His hazel eyes were enough to soak a broad's panties all on their own. He weighed in at a hefty two hundred pounds even. His solid build came from serving short bids in the juvenile prison system.

The howling wind caused him to squint as it smacked across his face. *Disrespectful as a muthafucka*, he thought. His earlobes felt raw and damn near ready to fall off. He'd lost his earmuffs a few weeks ago, and his only thoughts were of how much he'd really missed them. His dark brown ears were of a red hue. His fingers and toes felt numb.

He crossed the busy street of N. 35th and Vliet, nearly dropping his sacred package in a hurried attempt to make it back to his destination unseen and out of the cold. He breathed a sigh of relief and clutched the package tightly, securing it between his forearms and abdomen, trudging through the snow-covered roads until he reached Stevo's backdoor. He re-adjusted the package before beating on the door as the vapor from the bitterly cold winter escaped his dry, cracked lips.

Bam. Bam. Bam. Bam.

Stevo leaped from the couch and frowned, seizing the baseball bat beside it. He hurried up the back steps, stopping in front of the backdoor. The baseball bat was hoisted up against his shoulder as if he were up to bat in a game, and ready to swing for a home run. "Say, Joe, who the fuck beatin' on the door like they crazy?" He demanded. Stevo was five feet eleven inches tall with caramel skin and shoulder length dreads. He had a muscular frame that was built and always ready for war.

"Say, Joe, open up the muthafuckin' door. It's cold as a bitch out here!" Makaroni hollered, shaking.

A smile crept across Stevo's face. He sat the bat beside the door and pulled off the two-by-four that was used as a second line of defense against the many burglars and Jack Boys in the area. The city of Milwaukee had gotten terrible. With the economy declining like Donald Trump's approval ratings it felt like every man was out for himself, and most of the niggas that roamed the streets were playing for keeps, by any means.

Stevo pulled open the door, and Makaroni rushed inside hugging himself. He could feel the cold air coming from his right-hand man's body. A blast of the cold invaded the back hallway, sending chills all over him. He quickly closed the door, replacing the two-by-four to its original position.

Makaroni rushed down the back steps, into the basement. "Damn, nigga, what the fuck took you so long? A nigga prolly got frost bite 'n shit." He hugged himself tighter as his teeth chattered.

"Bruh, I came as fast as I could. You already know I would never leave you out there like that." Stevo replied, stepping further into the basement that was comprised of a couch, a small table, and a dryer. Stevo's mother didn't have a washer. It had broken down nearly two months back. Now they washed their clothes in the tub but had the blessing of drying them inside of the dryer, though it did very little to prevent the wrinkles from forming. He had a blue light bulb screwed inside of the socket. The bulb caused the entire basement to take upon the color of blue. "Did you get it?" Stevo could barely contain himself.

Makaroni had been blowing into his closed fists, all the while clutching the package in his left arm. He smiled. "Know that." He unzipped his black Bomber jacket that was filled with various holes from wear and tear. As soon as it was opened, he pulled the wrapped sawed-off shotgun from inside his coat. He knelt by the table and placed the sawed-off on top of it, slowly peeling back the layers of sheet from around it. "My aunty Bonnie punk ass husband didn't want to leave her bedroom. That's what took me so long. She left for work like two hours ago." He shook his head in frustration. "But it's all good. We got this bitch now though." He stood up and held the shotgun out for Stevo to admire.

Stevo smiled and came closer. The shotgun was all black. Where the barrel had been sawed off it looked silver, and just a tad bit crooked. "Let me hold that ma'fucka."

Makaroni handed him the shotgun and took a seat on the couch. "Yo, where the fuck is that half a blunt I had before I left?" He asked feeling a headache coming on.

Stevo was lost in a trance as he marveled at the sawed-off shotgun in his hands. It felt heavy, and cold. He held it out as if he were going to shoot a target, as goosebumps appeared all over his body. He knew that in his hands he held the power over life and death.

Makaroni jumped up. "Nigga, did you hear what the fuck I asked you?" There was silence. Stevo was in another world. "Stevo!"

Stevo snapped out of his zone. "What? Got-damn, nigga?" He held the shotgun at his side.

"Where the fuck is my half of blunt?" He questioned again, irritation in his tone.

"I smoked that bitch. My head was hurting. Plus, you was takin' too ma'fuckin' long. I got you though." Stevo went back to playing around with the shotgun. He held it in a firing position, and closed his right eye, aiming it at a random spot on the wall.

"Fuck you mean you smoked my shit, Stevo? That was the only Killa I had left to my name, nigga."

"Bruh, it's good. Now that we got this ma'fucka, we ain't finna be worrying about not having shit no more. Word up."

Makaroni ran his fingers in circles over his temples. Stevo was always pissing him off by doing things like that. The two had been the best of friends ever since they were three years old and living in the Village Housing Projects in the city of Chicago, Illinois.

Both of their mothers had been best friends and had attended high school together. They had got pregnant about the same time, and gave birth a few months apart. When Stevo's mother, Cassidy, decided to move out of the cold-hearted streets of Chicago, her best friend, Maisey, decided to follow suit weeks later, especially after Cassidy promised that Milwaukee, Wisconsin would be a fresh start with safer streets, and better paying jobs.

It only took both families a few months to see that Milwaukee, though smaller than Chicago, was just as deadly, if not worst at times. Both families struggled and had been leaning on each other for support ever since.

Makaroni sat on the couch and looked over at the ashtray. He found a small duck and picked it up. He sparked it and began to puff on it before it burned his fingers. He dropped it and closed his eyes. "Nigga, now what?" He asked, as calmly as he could.

"Now, we finna buss a few moves so we can make shit happen. I told you that I already got a few lil' licks lined up. All I needed was a piece. This ma'fucka finna make some noise." He held the weapon out again and nodded. He visualized pulling a kick-door with the gun. His heartbeat quickened. He couldn't wait to get things started.

Makaroni stood up. "Man, fuck waitin'. Let's go holler at them lil' young niggas up the block that be pushing that bunk ass weed. All they got in there is a weak ass Twenty-Two. We can hit they shit, and come away with their burner, and all the money they got in that ma'fucka. What you think?"

Before Stevo could answer the question, Cassidy crept down the steps, and peeked her head into the basement. She looked the two young men over and smiled. "I thought I heard noise down here. Y'all hungry?"

Stevo frowned. "Mama, what I tell you about comin' down here without announcing yo'self first? Damn, we could have been on any type of shit right now." Stevo snapped.

Cassidy smacked her lips. "Boy, what I tell you about thinking you have *rights* to any privacy when you live under my roof? On which bill is your name under? And how many of them ma'fuckas do you contribute to? Huh? I didn't think so."

"Here we go with this shit." Stevo turned his back to her.

"Yeah, you damn right here we go."

Makaroni slipped up next to Cassidy and slid his arms around her waist. She was only five feet two inches tall. Petite and gorgeous with her natural Creole yellow color, long, curly hair, and a southern body that, unbeknownst to Stevo, drove him crazy. Her eyes were honey brown, and she always smelled so good. "Hey, mama. How are you?" He hugged her, catching a whiff of her perfume.

Cassidy sunk into him, hugging him back, before stepping out of his arms. "I'm good, baby. How is Maisey? She ain't been on Facebook in a few days."

"She just been workin'. But she good though." He looked into her eyes and felt an odd feeling of excitement.

13

"Well, that's good to hear. You hungry?"

He nodded. "Ma'am. I'm hungry for whatever you cooked. You be throwin' down."

Cassidy laughed. Her perfume was now beginning to permeate the basement. "What about *you,* boy?"

Stevo turned around. "Yo, maybe when we get back. But we on something right now. Can you give us a minute?"

Cassidy stared at him for a moment. She closed her eyes, and took a deep breath. "You know what, Stevo, I'm not gon' let you ruin my night. The food is already done, and I'll make ya'll plates whenever you two get back." She waved him off, making her way up the stairs.

Makaroni's eyes were pinned to the ass that was stuffed inside the pair of tight denim jeans she had on. She was so thick that even in the jeans, her ass couldn't help but to jiggle a bit. The sight was tantalizing. He felt his piece getting hard. He had to remind himself that Cassidy was his right-hand man's mother.

"Nigga, let's go handle this business. I need to put a few dollars in my pocket." Stevo announced, picking up the shotgun. "How many bullets you got for this ma'fucka?"

"I don't know. I grabbed as many as I could. They in my coat over there. Load it, and let's roll."

Stevo sat down on the couch and proceeded to loaded up the shotgun. "I'm tired of her always throwing that punk shit in my face, Makaroni. On some real shit, as soon as I get enough bread to bounce from her crib, I'm up out dis ma'fucka. Believe that."

"Nigga, you trippin'. Yo mother love the fuck outta you. She don't ever get on that dumb shit with you unless you get on it with her first. You better cherish that woman."

"Fuck that. Nigga, that's for my pops to do. I already got my hands full with Keaira." Keaira was Stevo's main bitch, and baby mother. They had been together ever since he was fifteen years old.

"What you talking about?"

"Man, ever since she had my son, that bitch just been actin' real crazy. She on dis family shit, when that's the furthest thing from my mind. I can't see myself settling down with her or nobody else, no time soon. I'm just keepin' shit real." He finished loading the shotgun and laid it across his lap. "You know her brother Dexter fuckin' with them chickens now though. He always tryna put me on, but a few ma'fuckas done told me that he might be the Feds. That shit got me kind of nervous."

Makaroni sat down on the couch across from him. "Lil' bum ass Dexter fucking with birds now? Since when?"

"Since he started jamming with that Mexican bitch he just had a lil' girl with. Last time I saw him in South Ridge, that nigga was pushing a black Jaguar truck. Twenty-twenty edition, too. You know he be having that cake."

Makaroni stroked his chin hairs. "Yeah, well, why the fuck are we about to lay down these broke ass weed pushers when we can hit his ass on some real paper?"

Stevo snapped his neck to look at him. "Nigga, that's my baby mother brother. My son's uncle. I can't lay him down. That would be foul as hell."

"Yeah, you right. You would be foul. But I wouldn't. Let me hit his ass. I'll still buss everything down the middle with you. You already know how we get down. What do you say?"

Stevo thought about it for a minute. He thought about how Dexter had always been cool with him. How he had always tried to help him out by putting him on his feet. The man, though only slightly older than himself, had always treated him like a little brother that he loved. He didn't want to betray him as much as his pockets called for it. "N'all, bruh, we ain't on that shit. If we gon' fuck with Dexter, then it's gone be on the up and up. I could never hurt Keaira like that. That fool means the world to her. Plus, he paying all her bills. You know he gon' have to, 'cause I ain't." He stared at Makaroni with a serious look on his face. "Anyway, let's get the fuck up outta here and handle this business. I ain't got one red cent to my name."

Makaroni nodded, throwing on his jacket. "Aiight, well, I'ma let you have this argument. But holla at that nigga and see if he'll put us on. We twenty now; being broke ain't cute."

"Nigga, don't I know it." Stevo grabbed the shotgun and headed toward the backdoor. His ski mask was already inside of his coat pocket. *Time to get this money up*, he thought. He was tired of feeling like a bum. Tired of being broke without a pot to piss in nor a window to throw it out of. *Yeah, I'ma lay these niggas down, then I'ma get Dexter to fuck with us. If he ain't tryna look out for us, then I'ma have to roll with Makaroni plan. Any ma'fucka can get it. That's just how I feel.*

Chapter 2

Makaroni knocked on the side door to the weed spot and blew into his gloved hands. The temperature had dropped another five degrees. His cheeks were on fire. He stomped his right foot into the ground so he could get some sort of feeling to come back into it. His toes felt like they were about to snap off at any second. The wind blew, causing his clothes to wag in the wind. He lowered his head and knocked on the side door again.

The young Dope Boy came and opened the door a crack. "What's good, homie? What you tryna cop?" He asked trying his best to sound as tough as he could.

"Say, bruh, y'all still popping them fifty dollar zips?" Makaroni asked, feeling his adrenalin begin to course through his system.

"Yeah, dem bitches popping all day. Twenty-eight grams strong, straight Baby Dro. How many you looking for?"

"Let me get two. But I don't want all them seeds in my shit like y'all hit me wit' before." Makaroni said, fishing. In actuality he had never copped anything from the weed spot before. He had only heard about how the bud was coming seeded out. But he needed for the young dealer to think that he had copped from them before. That would establish a level of trust and regularity. If the Dope Boy thought that Makaroni had purchased his work before, he would be less likely to be nervous about serving him, or about becoming careless during their transaction.

"Say, homie, I don't know who served you before, but it wasn't me. My shit straight. I'ma give you fifty-six with a minimal amount of seeds. I got you." He assured Makaroni.

"Shit, if you coming like that, then hit me wit' three of them for the one-fifty." Makaroni urged. "Just make sure that shit good though."

"I got you. I'll be right back." He started to close the door.

"Wait a minute. Let me get that green."

Makaroni took a step closer. "Man, y'all got me last time. I need to see my shit this time before I purchase it. I'm sorry, homeboy. Plus, this ain't just my money. I'm throwing in with a few of my Day Ones."

The Dope Boy frowned. He opened the door wider to expose that he was carrying a .9 millimeter in his hand. He mugged Makaroni. Makaroni wondered where had gotten the pistol from. He was under the impression that the weed spot was only strapped with a .22. "Look, nigga, I just told you that I had yo ass. Ain't no mafucka finna play you." The slender teen said. "Either you finna give me that money or I'm finna slam this door in yo mafuckin' face. Which is it going to be?" He spat.

Makaroni held his hand up. "Aiight, nigga, damn. But you bet not be on no bullshit." He slid his hand into his pocket with the young Dope Boy watching him closely.

As Makaroni was getting ready to slide the dollar bills out, Stevo nudged him to the side, and cocked the shotgun, aiming it at the young Dope Boy. "Fuck nigga, break yo self; you already know what time it is."

The Dope Boy, in a haste, jumped back, and tried to slam the door. Makaroni rushed it, and bore through it like a running back burrowing through a crowd of linebackers to get his touchdown. The door flew open with a loud bang. The knob slammed into the wall and left a huge hole inside of it. The Dope Boy was on the third step, making his way back into the house when Makaroni tackled him to the stairs, and pulled him down them.

Stevo ran up the flight, and hopped over the struggling pair. He eased into the house. There was a loud stench of marijuana smoke. He lowered his eyes. The heat of the duplex felt good to him. His heart beat inside of his chest rapidly as he eased further inside of the weed Trap. After taking twenty steps he paused inside of the hallway that led to the living room. He looked down it, and saw two dudes sitting on the couch with remote controls in their hands. He could hear the sounds of Fortnite on the television screen. He dropped down as low as he could, and picked up the pace. Faster and faster. The floor of the hallway turned into carpet as he stepped into the living room and stood all the way up. "Everybody, get y'all punk ass on the ground. Break yo self! if I have to tell you again, I'm bussing this mafucka."

The remote controllers dropped quickly. Both men held up their hands, and slowly knelt to the floor. Once their they laid on their stomachs with their hands above their heads. Stevo rushed them, and went to work stripping them as he had done so many of his victims before.

**

Crunch! The Dope Boy brought his knee up and slammed it into Makaroni's nuts. "Bitch ass nigga!"

Makaroni dropped the gun he'd previously recovered from the Dope Boy. It bounced off of the third step and fell all the way back to the door that Makaroni had busted through. He fell against the banister. The Dope Boy rushed him, swinging as hard as he could, connecting with his jaw once, and then his left eye, stunning Makaroni. He swung again, and punched his jaw for the second time.

Makaroni felt dazed. He held on to the banister for a second. When he saw the Dope Boy jumping down the steps, headed for the .9 millimeter, he snapped out of it. He jumped down the stairs and landed right on his back. Grabbing him by the shirt and throwing him into the wall as hard as he could.

The Dope Boy's face smashed into the wall, banging his teeth. He felt it click, and then fall against his lip. Blood began to seep out of his mouth. He groaned in pain. He could feel the weight of Makaroni on top of him. He struggled to get up but couldn't.

Makaroni took a hold of the .9 millimeter, and held it to the back of the Dope Boy's head. "How much work y'all got in here? Huh?"

The Dope Boy groaned. "Nigga, fuck you. I ain't telling you shit. Kiss my ass."

"Oh, yeah." Makaroni raised the gun over his head and brought it down as hard and as fast as he could. The steel crashed into the Dope Boy's temple, and sunk inside of the tender flesh there. The Dope Boy hollered out in excruciating pain as blood oozed down the side of his face swiftly. "How much y'all got in here?" Makaroni asked again.

"Two pounds. Just two pounds. Now get the fuck off of me!" He whimpered.

"Where is it at? Huh?" Makaroni wrapped his arm around his throat. He squeezed, and pulled his neck backward. "Where is it?" He bounced up and down on his back. He could feel it popping. He released his hold just a bit. "Tell me!"

"In the Captain Crunch cereal boxes inside of the pantry. It's only six of them. That's where it's at."

"Good." Makaroni proceeded to choke him out. His jaw was hurting from where the Dope Boy rocked him twice. His nuts felt like they were still inside of his stomach. Makaroni wanted revenge. His anger was getting the best of him. He pulled backward, and squeezed as hard as he could. The Dope Boy's neck popped twice before Makaroni slammed his face in the floor, bussing it wide open. Makaroni stood up and

20

looked down on him. He saw that he was unmoving. He stomped him five hard times before disappearing into the house, leaving the Dope Boy lifeless.

***

Stevo stuffed the two pounds of bud into his black garbage bag, alongside the jewelry that he'd taken off of his victims. He tied the bag in a knot, then hoisted it over his shoulder. "Bruh, what you wanna do wit' these niggas?" He asked Makaroni.

Makaroni held the shotgun down on them. He had a million thoughts going through his head. He didn't think it would be smart to kill the pair. Nor would it have been smart to leave them alive either after how he'd taken the life of the other young hustler. He was caught between a rock and a hard place. "I don't know."

"You don't know? Aiight, fuck it. Let me make the decision for you then." He took the .9 off of his hip that Makaroni had given him, aimed it down, and cocked it. "Bye, niggas."

"Wait, man, please don't do th—"

Boom. Boom. Boom. Boom.

Makaroni stood back, and watched him finger fuck the .9 like a Savage. His bullets ripped them to shreds. Gunsmoke filled the air. Big puddles of burgundy blood formed under their bodies. The scent of burned flesh entered the atmosphere. Makaroni looked on, shaking as if he were freezing. But being cold had nothing to do with his shakes. It was the murders that were causing him to act the way that he was. The sight both excited and terrified him. He could only imagine the bad karma that it would bring. He didn't have room to give a fuck. He could only be ready for whatever came. He was tired of giving passes to niggas when they laid them down. Now it was all about the money and body count.

***

Cassidy looked over at Makaroni and laughed at the way he was sucking his fingers. She had her Avant playing through the speakers in the background. Was fresh from a shower, and happy that her mind could rest easy because her son Stevo was in the house safe and sound. "You want another piece of chicken, Makaroni?" She grabbed a big thigh, and placed it on his plate before he could answer.

"Thanks, ma." He responded, and started to douse it with Tabasco sauce.

"You're welcome, honey." She looked across the table at Stevo. "Boy, what's the matter with you?"

Stevo spooned up a nice portion of rice. "Nothing. I'm in my own lane. Why you fuckin' wit' me?"

"I'm not, I'm just asking what's up with you." She sat back, and looked him over. "Why you ain't touching yo chicken? What? You don't like it a something?"

"It's straight. You done did a better job before, but it is what it is."

"Aw." Cassidy was stomped. She didn't understand how their relationship could be so sour. The good Lord knew that she loved her son with all of her heart.

"Yo, I ain't gon' be in yo house forever. Soon, I'ma go out and make shit happen for myself. You better believe that. You ain't gon' always be able to throw me staying here in my face." He screwed up his upper lip, and mugged her.

"Boy, you still sitting over there dwelling on that?" She scooted back from the table, and picked up her dishes. Scraping the contents into the garbage, before rinsing the plate out. "Baby, as long as you are safe and sound, you can stay here as long as you want."

"Don't call me baby. That shit weird. And secondly, if that was the case, you wouldn't be throwing that shit in my face every chance you get." He stood up, and slammed his napkin into his plate.

Makaroni felt like getting up and bussing Stevo in his shit. He couldn't stand how disrespectful he was to his mother. It was the one thing that he hated about his homie. He wanted to interject but knew that it would be the wrong move.

"You know what, Stevo? Whenever you're ready to leave my shit, you can go. You are way too disrespectful to be staying in my home talking to me like this."

"This my pops' shit. You barely pay any bills yo self. So, if you wanna be technical, we on the same mafuckin' level. But it's all good though. I'm finna get my money up, and then I'ma be out of here. After I leave, I don't want you to say another mafuckin' word to me. You got that, Cassidy?"

She nodded, and turned her back to them. Tears sailed down her cheeks. "Okay, son. I wish you the best." She placed her dishes in the sink, and left the kitchen.

Stevo sat back down, and started to eat with a big smile on his face. He adjusted in his seat. Got up, and grabbed a Pepsi out of the refrigerator. "That's how you stand on a bitch."

"Nigga, what you just say?" Makaroni snapped.

Stevo popped the top on his Pepsi, and turned it up. He didn't feel like arguing with Makaroni. His homie had a habit of taking his mother's side as if she were an angel or something. So he continued to eat, ignoring him.

"Bruh, I love you and all of that shit, but the way you be handling yo mother gon' come back to haunt you one day. You only get one mother."

"I ain't trying to hear all that shit, Makaroni. You see how she be coming at me all sideways and shit. Nigga, I'm a young god. She need to approach, and handle me as such. It's as simple as that."

23

"Dawg, if you keep talking that stupid shit, I'm finna hit you in yo shit. That's on my moms."

"Fuck you, Makaroni. Fuck you, and Cassidy, nigga. I say what the fuck I wanna say. Ain't nobody gon' stop me from doing that."

"Oh yeah?"

"Yeah, nigga." He stuffed a piece of chicken into his mouth and chewed down on it. The crispy skin popped, and squirted perfectly seasoned flavor across his tongue.

"Dawg, let's go outside. On my mother, I'll beat yo tough ass right now for how you getting down on yo Queen. Fuck you wanna do?" Makaroni stood up, and wiped his fingers on a napkin. Grease from the chicken decorated the corners of his mouth.

Stevo looked up at him. "Nigga, if we go outside and knuckle up the way I'm feeling, somebody gon' die tonight. You sho you ready to risk that shit because of how I'm treating my old girl?"

"Yep? Let's get it."

"Aiight den." Stevo jumped up with his fist balled up. His fingernails were caked with chicken and Tabasco sauce.

Cassidy walked back into the kitchen, and stood in the middle of them. "Y'all ain't finna do this. We are a family." She turned to Stevo. "Son, I don't know what you are going through, but I hope it passes soon. I love you, and I forgive you." She walked over to Makaroni. "Son, why don't you go home for the night? Get you some sleep. I love you, and thank you." She kissed his cheek, and smiled at him, thankful that he would step up for her honor when she felt that he really didn't have to. She wished that her own son could love her as much.

"Yeah, nigga, take her advice. We been through a lot tonight. I'll fuck wit' you in the morning."

Makaroni mugged him for a long time. He ran his tongue over his teeth. Then he nodded. "Yeah, aiight, Ma, I'ma do just that. I love you, and hold ya head up. You are a Queen. Never forget that." He turned to Stevo. "Give me a few days. I gotta get my head right." He grabbed his portion of the lick, then left their home feeling angry, and extremely irritable. He couldn't believe how his right-hand treated Cassidy. He prayed that one day Stevo would grow up.

Ghost

Chapter 3

Tap. Tap. Tap. Tap. Maisey tapped on Makaroni's door for the third time, before twisting the knob, and pushing it inward. "Baby, wake up. I need you to come out here and talk some sense into your sister. Please."

Makaroni sat up in his bed, and rubbed his fists into his eyes. He felt groggy. He was still sleepy. He took his fists away, and opened his eyes just as a strong breeze came through the window, giving him imminent chills. He shivered. "Ma, what she tripping on?" He asked, throwing the blanket off of him. He stood up, and slipped into his jeans.

Montana came into the hallway close to his bedroom. "Mama, you ain't gotta wake him up. I'm finna figure this it out on my own. I'm tired of having to depend on everybody else. It's time that I get out here and make shit happen on my own." She announced, as she made her way down the hallway, talking to herself.

Maisey stood in the doorway with her head down. She shook it. "Sometimes I wish I could find y'all daddy and kick his ass. It's his fault that we going through all of this shit. Man, I hate him." She stepped away from the door, and went back to her room, slamming the big door.

Minutes later Makaroni stepped into the living room. Montana was pacing, still talking to herself. She couldn't believe how Devon would do her. She felt like a fool. She wanted to kill him, and even though she felt angry enough to think that she could actually follow through with the act, in actuality she knew that it was only spiteful thinking. She heard footsteps, and turned to see a shirtless Makaroni step into the living room. "Boy, I don't got time to be fucking wit' you right now."

The first thing that Makaroni noticed about his sister was the fact that she had a black eye. Her left eye was not only black, but it was swollen. He closed the distance between them quick, and snatched her up. He pinned her to the wall, and held her by her chin. "Who did this shit to you?"

Montana tried to wiggle out of his embrace. "Let me go, Mack. What's the matter with you?"

Makaroni tightened his grip on Montana. "Yo, I'ma ask you again. Who did this shit to you? Tell me."

She closed her eyes and maintained her silence. She knew that her brother was off of his rocker. His temper was lethal. Even though he was born first, and only minutes apart, he treated her as if she were his kid sister. She didn't like that at times.

"Montana, who the fuck did this shit to you?"

She struggled against him, and then managed to break free of his grip after he loosened it only slightly. "Let me go, Makaroni. You're not my damn daddy. Fuck." She rubbed her chin, mugging him.

He stepped into her face. She took a step back. He took another step forward. "Was it that nigga Devon that did this shit, huh? You fuckin wit' that fake ass pimp again?" He snapped.

She lowered her head. "Shut up. I don't got time for this this right now." She walked away from him, and sat on the couch. Her head remained lowered. She found a discolored spot on the carpet, and zoomed into it.

Makaroni sat across from her. "Montana, holler at me, sis. Look, I apologize for snatching you up. But I love you. I don't want no nigga putting his hands on you. So, who did this shit?"

Montana was five feet six inches tall. Caramel skinned, with brown eyes. Her hair was shoulder length. She kept it permed, and silky. She glared at him, after placing a tuft of her hair behind her right earlobe. "Makaroni, I don't need you fighting my battles, nigga. I'm strong. I see what happened to my face. I'll take care of this. I ain't gon' let him get away with it."

Makaroni was clenching his jaw muscles harder and harder. He loved his sister with all of his soul. His mother as well. The trio had been through so much together, had prevailed for the most part. Because of their past struggles, Montana suffered from severe depression and anxiety. She had a low self-worth, and tended to hang on to low-life men that she felt she needed to validate her purposes in life. This drove Makaroni crazy. Deep down he felt that she was the way she was because of how their father up and left them in the trenches so that he could become a constant father to his second family that he had put up in a suburb of Milwaukee called Wauwatosa.

Makaroni slid on the couch beside her. He placed his arm around her shoulder. "Montana, I ain't trying to fight your battle, but you already know that I ain't finna go for nobody putting their hands on you. So, tell me what the deal is, and let me finish this nigga so we can move on."

She eased away from him. She stood up. "I got it this time, Makaroni. Stay the fuck out of my life. You don't own me. You need to get yo own shit together. You the only nigga I know besides Stevo that's twenty and still living wit' his mama. That's bum shit." She rolled her eyes. "Ain't nobody got respect for you." She walked away from him. "Mind yo own business. I ain't gon' tell you again."

Makaroni sat on the couch feeling like a straight loser. Her words continued to play over and over in his head. He knew she was right. He was a bum. He didn't have nothing going on for himself. He'd dropped out of school at sixteen. Had been in and out of the juvenile system ever since. On top of that, he had never seen more than two thousand dollars. He felt sick. "Shit ain't gon' always be this way. Mark those words. A mafucka just down right now." He said out loud to himself.

***

Stevo slammed his fist against the side of the beat up old 1987 Chevy Caprice Classic. He walked to the middle of the street and tried to calm down. Sometimes his temper was so bad that it caused him to feel dizzy. Winter smoke came from his mouth and nostrils. The wind howled, and blew around a Walmart shopping bag that had been left in the middle of the street.

Makaroni stepped out of the car. He zipped his Bomber jacket all the way up to his Adam's Apple. "Nigga, you getting all mad and shit ain't gon' make this mafucka start up. Maybe it's just popped this time." He came and looked under the hood, although he had no idea how things functioned under there.

Stevo came and stood beside him. "Dawg, I'm so tired of this shit, Mack. Fuck, nigga. Life is hard as a bitch. Then it seem like everywhere I go, it's a mafucka that's constantly reminding me of how fucked up I really am."

Makaroni flinched as the wind blew harshly. He closed his eyes and sniffled. "Me too, dawg. We gotta figure some shit out. My sister tried to go on me today."

Stevo went back to messing with the car's alternator. "Yeah, how she do that?" He asked ignoring the stinging coming from his earlobes. They were bright pink.

Makaroni got as far under the hood as he could without getting into his way. "Dawg, she say we the only two niggas she know that is twenty or better that's still living with our mothers. Called me a bum and all type of shit."

Stevo stood up and tightened the cap on the oil, before jiggling the two cable wires that were connected to the battery. They felt frozen. "What made her go on you like that?"

Makaroni sighed. "Some nigga blacked her eye. Got her walking around looking all crazy and shit. You already know what I wanted to do to the nigga. She shot that shit down. Said she can take care of herself. Then she got to attacking me all verbal and shit. What's crazy is that everything she said only hurt me because it was true. Right now, man, we are some bums."

Stevo was hunched over. He mugged him for what seemed like a long time. Then his face went softer. "Yeah, I guess you right."

Makaroni shook his head. He couldn't imagine what it was that he could be doing. He hated school even though he had tried his best to not feel that way. He was street smart. Book smarts was a whole other animal to him. He felt that nobody would hire him for a job, and even if they did, he wasn't sure that he could work anybody's nine to five. That seemed like slavery to him. So, he was stuck.

Stevo didn't care about nothing but fast money. Unlike Makaroni, he had never entertained the thought of trying in school. He wanted what he wanted instantly. Hard work was a fucking joke to him.

"Yo, Stevo, look up!" Makaroni hollered.

Before Stevo could pull his head from under the hood of his Caprice, Stacy, and two of his young killas were standing outside of his Yukon with a gun in each of their hands. Stacy was five feet five inches tall. Dark skimmed, with short dreads that were all over his head. He had tattoos all over his face. Most of them were money symbols, and stars. He walked up to Stevo and Makaroni, stopping short. His hittas behind him. "Say, Mane, my lil' nigga's weed spot got hit around the corner. You two niggas know anything about that?" He asked with a mouth full of gold.

Stevo dropped his oil rag, and stepped forward. "N'all, nigga, we don't. We don't give no fuck either." He snapped.

Makaroni pulled Stevo back. "Chill, homie." He mugged Stacy. "N'all we don't know nothin' about no weed spot getting hit. Keep that shit moving."

Stacy cocked his pistol. "N'all, nigga, that shit ain't that easy. You pussy mafuckas know somethin'." He looked over his shoulder. "Say, bruh, search these niggas."

"Search who? You ain't searching shit over here." Stevo snapped. He shook Makaroni off of him, and went to reach for his .9 millimeter that they had taken from the robbery, but forgot that he had left it in his parents' basement under the couch.

Stacy stuck the .40 Glock under his chin, and cocked the hammer. "Bitch, don't move or I'ma finna blow yo shit off. You either." He aimed his other .40 Glock at Makaroni.

Makaroni threw his hands up in the air. "Aiight, bruh. Y'all do what y'all gotta do." He felt like a pussy for real. A man having his gun pinned on you and invading your space was one of the worst feelings in the world to him.

Stevo stood still, mugging Stacy. They had always had beef ever since they were in high school. Stevo had fucked and taken Keaira away from Stacy. This was before Stacy's older brother Savage had been indicted. It was rumored that Savage had left Stacy with over four bricks of coke, and fifty thousand dollars. Stacy was having major chips in the game now, and had Dope Boys working for him all over the city. Like Makaroni and Stevo, he had just turned twenty years old.

Stacy smiled. His eyes never left Stevo's as his Hittas patted him down, turning his pockets inside out. "Nigga, you make one false move I'ma put yo blood all over this snow." He promised.

Stevo swallowed his spit. He began to shake. Something was telling him to swing and break Stacy's jaw. He hated the man. He disliked being treated as if he were nothing more than trash. This was his hood. Wasn't nobody supposed to be trying to treat him like a sucka. Yet there Stacy was.

Makaroni's pockets were turned inside out. One of the Hittas slammed him on the car's truck, and pressed his gun to the back of his head. He heard the hammer cock back. "Stacy, this broke ass nigga ain't got shit on him. What you want me to do wit' him?"

Stevo wound up in the same position. Stacy had both guns pointed to his jaw. "Strip him. I want both of these niggas ass naked. Now." Stacy demanded.

Makaroni kept his mouth closed as he was stripped out of his clothes. When he was ass naked, the cold attacked him. The Hitta that had stripped him went and stood beside Stacy with Makaroni's clothes, and his gun still trained on him. Next came the Hitta that had stripped Stevo.

Stacy backed up laughing. "Aiight, niggas. Y'all got to the count of three to run as far and as fast as you can. But when I get to three, me and my niggas bussing with no regard. Aiight? One..."

Stevo took off running. Makaroni was right on his heels. They got to the middle of the block before Stacy and his goons got to bussing back to back. The sound of the gunshots resonated loudly in the afternoon.

Makaroni somehow sped up and passed Stevo. He got to the park that was at the end of Stevo's street, and ran across it. Trekking as fast as he could. His lungs felt raw. It seemed as if he were inhaling ice cubes one after the other. His heart was beating so fast that it hurt. He looked over his shoulder to see Stevo ten yards behind him. Stevo looked backward, and tripped. He face-planted.

Stacy brought is Yukon to a halt. He jumped out of it with his killas in tow. They stopped and let off eleven rounds a piece. The bullets whizzed past both Stevo and Makaroni. Stevo jumped up with his nose bleeding. He ran as fast as he could across the snow. His asthma wreaking havoc on his lungs.

Both men made it all the way to 27th and Lisbon. Once there, they ran behind the BP gas station, and took the alley. Now their fast sprinting had been reduced to a mere jog. They found a garage and huddled inside of it. Breathing hard. Stevo fell to his knees, coughing and purging his guts. His chest felt like it was being beat on by a massive gorilla.

Makaroni stood with his back against the garage wall. Tears came down his cheeks from the cold, and from his anger. "I'm tired of this shit!" He snapped.

Stevo laid on his back. The garage was filthy. It smelled like motor oil and feces. Bums had been using it for weeks as a bathroom. "I'm killing Stacy, bruh. If. If." He began to cough, and hack up spit. He came to his knees to get it all out.

Makaroni stood, watching him. "I already know."

Stevo swallowed his spit, determined to finish what he was trying to say. "If it's the last thing I do."

Chapter 4

Stevo sat on the couch, and held his one-year old son, Steven, in his arms. He took the bottle off of the coffee table, and helped him to drink the breast milk Keaira had placed inside of it. He felt good in his arms. He smelled of baby lotion. Steven's hair was curling up nicely. Stevo was proud of that.

Keaira stepped into the living room with her work bag hoisted over her shoulder. "Well, I'm off to work. I should be back around eleven tonight because I gotta wait for Kelly to get off. I mean, unless you wanna come and pick me up." She batted her eyelashes at him.

Stevo mugged her. "Shorty, I done already told ya ass that my whip is fucked up. How would I possibly be able to pick you up?" He was frustrated.

Keaira placed her hand on her hip. She stood before him dressed in her blue nursing home uniform. "Why every time you come over here you always gotta have a attitude? Huh?"

"Keaira, gone. I ain't finna do this shit with you right now. I got a lot of shit on my mind." He looked down at Steven and saw that he was already falling asleep.

"Do what with me?" She asked, pressing the issue.

He mugged her. "Bitch, stop playing wit' me and take yo ass to work. Straight up."

She gasped. "Bitch? Really? Nigga, I ain't the one got stripped ass naked in the cold a few weeks ago. That would be you. Second to that. When are you putting in your child support?"

"Child support for what, Keaira? Everything you ask for when it comes to him, I make sure you get it. Fuck am I giving you shit throughout the month for if I'ma have to pay child support anyway? That shit don't make no sense." He kissed

Steven. "And far as Stacy go, bitch, you gon' read about him on the news, soon as I catch his punk ass."

Keaira dismissed his last statement. "Wait, so you think because you be giving me twenty dollars here and there that it's enough to provide for a whole ass child? Really?"

"Hell yeah. All he need to do is eat. That shit come out of your titties. That's free. He got plenty outfits. Fuck more he need?"

Kandace stepped into the house with her earbuds in her ears and bookbag over her shoulder. When she saw that Stevo was present, she rushed over to the couch and kissed him on the cheek. "Hey, big bro. 'Bout time you brought yo butt over here." Kandace was Keaira's baby sister. Both looked damn near identical. Light skinned, with hazel eyes, and beautiful faces. Keaira was five feet five inches tall. Kandace was five feet two. Keaira weighed a hundred and forty pounds. She had big breasts and an ass to match. Kandace was small up top, but her lower half made up for what her top was missing.

Stevo hugged Kandace with one arm. "Hey, lil' one. I'ma be here all night, so we can catch up."

"Aiight, I'ma finna go knock out my homework so we can chill until you leave." She kissed him on the cheek again, then left the living room.

Kelly blew her horn to signal to Keaira that it was time to go. Keaira pulled the curtain back and held up one finger. She stepped in front of Stevo. "Nigga, you need to get yo shit together. I ain't the only one that should be going to work right now. It takes two to provide for a child. You dropping the ball. Big time." She grabbed her coat off of the hook, and slid into it.

"Bitch, you gon' be late." He quipped.

She stood mugging him. "Worst decision I could've ever made was screwing you without a rubber. I love my son, but he could've came from anybody else."

Stevo stood up. Steven was already sleep in his arms. "Shorty, say that shit again."

Keaira's eyes grew as big as snowballs. "Look, just make sure you give him a bath before the night is out. I gotta go." She opened the front door, and closed it behind her. She shook her head all the way to Kelly's car, thinking about how trifling her baby daddy was.

Stevo stood there holding his son. He closed his eyes, and took a deep breath. Once again, his manhood had been bruised. He was so tired of hearing of his stature in society. It was beginning to make him feel like snapping out. He slowly opened his eyes just as Kandace stepped from her bedroom and into the kitchen. She was wearing a thin pair of pink lace booty shorts that were all up inside of her crack. Above those was a small white beater. Stevo looked down to Steven again. He saw that he was out, and smiled. He walked him into Keaira's room, and lowered him into the baby crib there, after kissing him on the forehead. He placed his pacifier inside of his mouth. Then eased out of the room.

When he got to Kandace's bedroom door, he found it slightly ajar. He nudged it just a bit more, and peeked inside. She lay on her stomach on top of the bed, typing away on her laptop. Earbuds in her ears, nodding to the music. Stevo's eyes glanced down her body. Now the shorts were so far inside of her ass crack that her yellow cheeks were fully exposed. Her knees were slightly spaced enough for him to make out her camel toe from the back. He felt his dick getting hard. She moved in the bed to grab a pen that was just to left of her computer. Stevo watched her thick cheeks jiggle like Jell-o.

He eased into the room, and closed the door behind him. His piece was jumping like crazy inside of his pants. He got as close to her as he possibly could, before lowering his face right between her thick thighs. Once there, he held her ass cheeks inside of his big hands, and pulled them apart. Her yellow sex lips hung out of the crotch band on each side. The lips had no trace of hair on them. Kandace jumped in fear after feeling him touch her. Before she could do more than that, Stevo had yanked her material to the side, and was sucking her pussy lips from the back. His long tongue roamed up and down her young slit, searching for her inner essence. He found her clitoris and sucked on it.

Kandace arched her back, and moaned. She tried to come to her knees. Stevo prevented that by placing his forearm into the small of her back. She looked over her shoulder to see his dreads. "Stevo?" She moaned again. His tongue traveled deep into her kitten. "Mmm. What are you doing?"

Stevo flipped her over, and spread her thighs. He ripped her panties from her with one tug. Her yellow pussy was now on full display. Both sex lips were engorged. Her nipples poked through her beater. He could make out the dark brown areolas. Though Kandace was young, she was strapped to him. He rubbed her pussy. Still tasting her on his tongue. "Damn, Kandace, I don't know how you done got this thick. You fuckin wit' one of them niggas out there?" He slipped a digit through her folds. Her pussy was leaking like a faucet.

She was still in shock. She couldn't believe that Stevo was touching her in the way that he was. He had always been nothing more than like an older brother to her. She didn't know what to do. "My mama don't let me have no boyfriends. She too strict."

Stevo took his wet finger and sucked it into his mouth. Her taste was savory. Just by putting a finger up there, he could tell that her cat had never been hit. That made him start to shake. Words from Keaira kept replaying themselves over in his mind. "I'm saying, Kandace. You my lil' baby though, right?" He proceeded to rub her lips again.

She nodded. "Yeah. Why you ask me that?"

He lowered himself until his face rested on her thigh. His fingers played through her wetness. "Because it's for me to take care of my lil' baby. You know I got you." He pushed her knees to her chest, and proceeded to eat her kitten hungrily. Sucking the lips. He ran his tongue in circles around her erect clitoris.

"Mmm. Mmm. Stevo. Big bruh. You... Mmm-a." She laid back, and squeezed her own breasts. She pulled her nipples that were so hard that they were hurting her. When she thought about what she was doing, she dropped her hands away, and moaned at the top of her lungs. It felt so good that she could barely breathe. She bucked three times, screamed, then came all over his mouth, humping into his face.

Stevo kept licking and sucking. His face was covered with her sexual secretions. Her scent drove him crazy. She smelled just like her sister when her own passions brought her over the edge. Their scents were nearly identical, yet Kandace smelled and tasted fresher. He waited for her to cum again before he sat back on his haunches, and played with her pussy with his fingers.

Kandace opened her thighs wide as she laid on her back. She didn't know what she expected to come next. She had never had sex before. She had always been too afraid. Too worried that her mother would find out. But Stevo had her pussy on fire. She was down to do anything.

Stevo stood on the side of the bed and pulled his long piece out. It sprung up like a brown cucumber. Veins decorated the length of it. He stroked it while he looked at her young kitten.

"Shorty, you lucky yo lil' ass so little. Straight up." He pulled her closer to him, and sped up his stroking, eyeing her gap the whole time. He imagined it being so tight that he couldn't get in. He knew it was hot. His tongue had told him that. "Damn, you lucky you a lil', shorty. Open them lips for me, and just let me see that pink."

Kandace followed his commands. Her cum was oozing out of her like never before. She had played with her button a bunch of times, but she had never felt like Stevo made her feel. Even though she was scared, she was feening for more of that feeling. "I ain't little." She opened her pussy lips wider, and rubbed around her clitoris.

Stevo felt like he was seconds away from cuming. "Yes, you is." He stopped. His dick jumped. "Girl, I could catch a case fuckin wit' yo lil' ass."

"Ain't nobody gon' say nothing. Dang, you think I'ma snitch a somethin?" She sat up, and tried to pull him down. "Big bruh, I need some. Everybody in my school already doing it. My mama won't let me do nothing. I'm always here. Smack dab in my room." She took a hold of his dick. "Keaira ain't gon' find out."

Stevo shivered as her little hand wrapped around his piece. "Stroke it, den."

She followed his commands. She licked her lips. "Do you trust me?"

"I don't trust nobody." He closed his eyes.

She sucked him into her mouth and got to slurping him like she saw all of the girls do in the porno movies when she used Keaira's phone. The fact that she was sucking her sister's baby daddy's dick only added to the spice of it all. She sucked faster.

Stevo grabbed a handful of her hair. He stroked her mouth. She gagged around him. He kept fucking. When he felt like he was about to cum, he pulled away from her. "Shorty, lay yo lil' ass back."

She scooted back, and opened her thighs. "You finna do it to me? Huh?" She was both excited and scared.

Stevo got between her thighs. He lowered himself. Took a hold of his pipe, and opened her pussy lips. "Damn, I wanna fuck you so bad, but I know you can't handle this grown shit."

"Yes, I can. You just think I'm still a baby."

He rested his dick head between her sex lips and moved it up and down without going deep inside of her. She whimpered, and dug her nails into his back. Her thick thighs wrapped around his waist. He juiced her faster and faster. Bumping her clitoris, feeling her lips wrap around his manhood nearly searing him.

"Mmm. Mmm. Mmm. Stevo. Stevo. Unnnnnnnnn-yes!" Kandace screamed, before cuming. She humped upward.

Stevo slipped a few inches inside of her. That was too much. He pulled out, and started to cum all over her kitty lips. She continued to hump upward, rubbing her cat all over his head while he spat his seed over her. It felt hot, and each drop drove her insane.

Ghost

Chapter 5

Makaroni was trekking through the snow on his way to Stevo's house when he heard *beep, beep.* He stopped in his tracks, and shielded his eyes from the falling snow to see who had beeped at him.

Kiana pulled her G Wagon beside him, and lowered her window. "What it do, Playboy? I see you still using those feet to get around everywhere." She smiled. Kiana was Thai and Black. She stood at five feet even, weighed in at a small a hundred and ten pounds. They had gone to high school together, and no matter how many times Makaroni had come at her, she had never given him the time of the day. He felt that she must've thought that he was cool enough to kick it with, but not cool enough to date. For the reason his feelings toward her were bittersweet.

Makaroni stepped to her passenger window. "What's good, girl?"

She turned down her music. Her thick lips were shimmering. They were painted heavy with Maybelline lip gloss. "I'm up here for a few weeks visiting from Miami. I was strolling through about to head down to the Bradley Center to watch the Bucks in action. That's when I saw you walking through all of this snow. Boy, you still ain't got a whip yet?" She gave him a serious look.

Makaroni felt like he'd been shot with a gun. He shifted uncomfortably as he leaned into her passenger's window. "N'all, but I'm working on it." He cleared his throat to break the silence. "I see you rolling a G Wagon, though. You got yo chips all the way up now, huh?"

"I'm doing okay." She sat back in her driver's seat just as a big city bus drove past them, making a bunch of noise. Its wheels kicked up a nasty amount of slushy black snow. "What's up with you though?"

He shrugged. "I don't know. Still trying to figure some shit out, that's all." He pulled his collar up further to cover his cheeks.

"Well, I was supposed to take my sister Kim to the game with me, but she ain't nowhere to be found. I think she sniffing up behind her nigga a something. But it's all good. I got two floor-seats if you wanna come and watch the game with me." She raised her right eyebrow. "I mean, if you ain't doing nothin' else. Maybe we can catch up a lil' bit."

The cold wind blew into the side of Makaroni's face again. He braced himself, and started to shake. He was still eight blocks away from Stevo's crib. Snow began to descend from the sky. He didn't want to make that journey, especially after feeling the heat drifting out of Kiana's warm wagon. He took a second to think about the fact that he only had five dollars to his name. He knew how expensive the Bradley Center was. Everything cost at least ten dollars or better. He winced in irritation. "Look, I would love to come out and fuck wit' you right quick, but I'm screwed up. My pockets on empty."

She snickered. "Mack, it's all good. I got you. I know shit hard out here for everybody. Besides, I'm inviting you out. That mean that it's my treat."

He couldn't even look her in the eyes. His pride was getting the better of him. "Shorty, why you want me to roll wit' you so bad anyway?"

Kiana looked into his handsome brown skinned face and saw potential. She heard about how Makaroni got down in the streets. She'd watched him fight two big seniors at their high school when he was only in the ninth grade for disrespecting his sister Montana. He'd whooped them real bad, and had gotten suspended from school. She knew he was a goon at heart.

A goon that she could use by her side. She popped the locks. "You rolling a what?"

Makaroni sighed, and grabbed the handle to the door. "Yeah, let's get it."

***

"Nigga, why you gotta get all of the cheap shit? Let's get these Huggies Pampers right here. Damn." Keaira snapped grabbing the Pampers and walking them toward the shopping cart.

Stevo ignored her. He grabbed a twenty-four pack of cheap Pampers that just read Diapers on the front of them. "Shorty, he a be cool with these right here. These the same mafuckin' deals but they just got a different name from that shit you got in your hand. You just paying for the brand name. Why can't you see that?" He asked getting irritated. He placed them inside of the buggy.

Keaira walked to the shopping cart, snatched the cheap diapers out, and slung them to the floor. "Nigga, my son ain't putting that shit on his body. If yo broke ass ain't gon' drop the chips so he can get a decent pack of Pampers then I'll buy this shit myself." She glared at him, and pushed the cart away from him.

Stevo stood in the aisle with his heart pounding in his chest. He clenched his fists over and over. He lowered his head and tried to calm down. As usual Keaira had him amped up. He felt like snapping out.

Keaira placed the groceries on to the Walmart check-out counter first. The groceries rolled past on a conveyer belt. The bagger picked up each item one by one and placed them inside of the bag. After paying for the groceries with her Link For Stamp card she got ready to swipe her debit card so she could pay for the Pampers, and the cat food that she'd picked up.

Stevo bumped her out of the way and handed the cashier a twenty-dollar bill. It was his last twenty. The cashier took it and added up the costs. The total came to twenty-three dollars even. He dug in his pockets for any form of currency and came up with none.

Keaira stood back looking him over. She couldn't believe the display that she saw in front of her. How could any man not have enough to fit the bill for his child's Pampers? She was grossed out. She felt like it was equivalent to watching a person eat their own booger.

"Yo, I'ma let her pay for that cat food. I don't even like cats anyway." He laughed.

"So, then you don't want the Purina?" The heavy-set Black woman asked.

"N'all, just the Pampers. How much is that?"

She deducted the cat food. "That'll be nineteen seventy-five."

"Aiight, cool." Stevo felt like shit. He watched the cashier personally wrap the Pampers. She handed them to him.

Keaira waited for him to walk through the check-out counter before she handed the cashier her debit card. "Girl, swipe that card for me. I gotta make sure my cat eat tonight." She laughed to lighten the mood.

The cashier did as she was told and handed the card back to Keaira. "Here you are, ma'am. Please have a good night."

"Thank you."

Stevo pushed the cart into the snowy parking lot. It was just after seven at night. The sun had already set. There were two snowplows removing the snow from the lot. He got to the back of his Chevy Caprice Classic that seemed to be acting right for the moment and popped the trunk. One by one he loaded the groceries into the back of the trunk.

Keaira slowly walked up to the car texting on her phone. She stopped for a moment to see Stevo had loaded up all of the bags into his car. She felt it was the least he could do. She rolled her eyes and got into the passenger's seat.

Stevo closed his trunk. He got into the car and closed the door. He turned on the ignition. He let his seat back, then with blazing speed he reached across the seat and took a hold of Keaira's throat. First with his left hand, and then with his right. He squeezed as hard as he could while she beat at his hands. She choked and hacked. Struggling to breathe. "Bitch, I told you about embarrassing me in public. I told you about yo mouth. I told you about yo attitude. Well, you gon' respect me." He squeezed harder and harder.

Keaira's eyes were bugged out of her head. She couldn't believe that this was happening to her. She prayed that it would stop. Prayed that he would come to his senses.

Stevo closed his eyes. The sounds of her choking aroused him. She beat at him as hard as she could. Then she took her nails and dug them into his neck. He exhaled with a sudden case of euphoria. He imagined her as a corpse and smiled, choking harder.

***

"Yo, when they start calling the Bradley Center the Fiserv Forum?" Kiana asked as they eased through the crowd with their food. She took the steps that led down to the floor-seats.

"It's been a short minute now. Didn't they have the name of the arena on your tickets?"

She kept walking until she found their lone seats, sat, and slowly placed her food in her lap. The basketball game had just started. They were only two minutes into the first quarter. The sounds of sneakers squeaking on the hardwood floor was loud in the arena coupled with cheers from the crowd, and the announcer urging the stadium to make some noise. "I had these tickets in Will Call for a few months now. My Pops got season tickets, but he's always traveling so he rarely makes any of the games."

Makaroni settled next to her. He felt odd putting the food that she'd bought on his lap. One of the worst feelings to him was that of feeling like a scrub. "Good looking on the tickets and shit. The food too. When I get right, I'ma make sure I hit yo hand back for what you paid for everything."

She laughed. "Boy, let it go. The tickets are a gift from my father. The food ain't run me nothing but a few pennies. It's good. Tell me why a nigga can take a female out every day of the week and she appreciate that. But when a woman take a man out, y'all always gotta feel emasculated? That don't make no sense." She shook her head, squirted hand sanitizer into her palm. She rubbed it around and handed the bottle to Makaroni.

He did the same thing. "It ain't that. I'm just used to having my own. And regardless of what you talking about, I am gon' pay you back. Deal wit' it."

She crunched down on a Nacho and held up her hand in submission. Then she was laughing. "N'all, it's all good. If that's what you wanna do, then do that." She looked out at the game. Giannis, the star forward for the Milwaukee Bucks, crossed two defensive players, and dunked on both of them. He flexed in their face and ran down the court with a mug on his grill. Kiana clapped. "That's my boy right there."

Makaroni nodded. He wasn't with holding another man's dick, but he had to admit that Giannis was the best player in the NBA. He scanned the packed arena. From the floor he felt like a boss. He knew that sitting in the best seats was where he was supposed to be. It felt right.

"Makaroni, would you be mad if I told you that I had a hidden agenda for asking you to come down here with me tonight?" She picked up her Pepsi and took a long drink from the straw.

He glanced at her from the corners of his eyes. "I figured as much. Tell me what's good."

"You remember my father, Deacon, right?"

Makaroni nodded. Deacon had been a Milwaukee legend. He was the first Dope Boy from their city that made a million dollars in the game. That was back in the early nineties. After he'd made that million, he paid his way through college and became a stockbroker on Wall Street. From there he ventured off into real estate and became a mogul. "Yeah, I remember yo old man. What about him?"

Kiana sucked on her bottom lip. "He need a few favors. Favors that I think if you fulfill them that will turn out to be quite lucrative for you and your crew."

"Crew? I ain't got no ma'fuckin' crew. Only person I fuck wit' is Stevo. It's always been like that."

"Yeah, well, if you do things the right way it'll be beneficial for him too. You down to find out what he want?" She asked, eating another cheesy Nacho.

Makaroni looked over at her just as Brooke Lopez hit a three-pointer from the top of the key. He threw his arms up. The crowd went crazy. "What type of money are we talking about?"

"All you gotta tell me is that you're interested, and that you are willing to travel."

"Travel where?"

"That don't matter. Is that a yes to both or not?" She sat her food on the floor.

"As long as yo old man with helping me and my nigga come from out of this struggle then I'm 'bout whatever."

She sat back and crossed her thighs. "Okay, den it's on. Let me work my magic." She slurped her drink some more.

"You gon' tell me why you doing this again?" Makaroni asked.

"Nope. That's for me to know and for you to find out."

***

Stevo pulled into the alley behind his house in a panic. He threw the car in park and hopped out. He rushed around to the passenger's door and pulled it open. Grabbed Keaira by the shoulders and pulled her to the snowy ground. Once there he knelt in the snow and tapped her on the side of the cheek. "Shorty, wake yo ass up. Come on now. Please." He slapped her.

Keaira was unresponsive. Her neck was bright red and slowly turning purple. She laid out as flat as a board. The wind whipped her hair across her face.

Stevo looked down at her and didn't know what to do. He was sure she was dead. He killed his son's mother. He wondered what he was going to do. He stood up and paced in front of her body. Sweat dripped down the side of his face. "Fuck. What did I do?" The wind blew, nearly knocking him over. He knelt back down. He pinched her nose and blew into her mouth until her chest rose. Then he began to administer CPR in a frenzy.

Two bums stuck their heads out of a garage. They watched Stevo in action, sure that Keaira had overdosed off some sort of drug. Snow continued to fall from the sky. It was turning out to be one of the coldest November's on record.

Stevo blew into her mouth again. Then he was doing chest compressions over and over. He stopped to look down at Keaira. Still she did not move. He felt his heart drop. "Got-damn. Come on, bitch!" He slammed his fist down as hard as he could directly into the center of her chest. The impact caused her to roll onto her side, coughing up a storm. The sound sent Stevo to his feet. He was in a state of relief.

Keaira continued to cough and cry at the same time. She curled into a ball. "What did you do to me, Stevo?" More coughing. "What did you do?"

Stevo kneeled. "I'm sorry, baby. I swear I am. I don't know what got into me. I just snapped."

Keaira rolled to her butt and stood up on wobbly legs. "I hate you, Stevo. I swear I hate yo fuckin guts. You could've killed me!" She took off running toward his house. Then when she saw where she was, she stopped in her tracks and fell to her knees crying her heart out. "I hate you so much. You could've taken me from my baby. How could you do this to us?"

Stevo stood there for a long time, looking her over. He didn't know what to say or do. Finally, he got back into his car and slammed the doors. Then he was storming down the alley, leaving Keaira standing there in the freezing cold.

Ghost

Chapter 6

"Man, when we supposed to be meeting up with this old ass nigga?" Stevo asked before turning a bottle of Hennessey up. He guzzled as if he was thirsty. The brown liquor burned his throat. It felt good to him. He could even feel the burning sensations in his nose.

Makaroni sat on the back-porch steps with a blunt in his hand. Every time the wind blew, it caused for the cherry on the blunt to eat up the sides of the cigar. He cuffed it to prevent it from messing up too much. "In two days, bruh. We gon' roll down to Miami to meet up with him." Makaroni took a strong pull from the blunt and inhaled. He passed it to Stevo.

"What the fuck he want with us though? We don't even know that stud like that." Stevo didn't like, nor did he trust people that he didn't know. He felt like the world was against him. He'd felt that way ever since he was ten years old and his fifth-grade teacher told him that he would never be nothing more than a drug dealing gang banger with a bad temper.

"All I know is that Kiana saying whatever he want with us that it's about to put some dough in our pockets, so I'm all in. You need to be too. I know you're tired of mafuckas calling you a bum, or a poor excuse for a man."

Stevo blew his smoke to the air. "Wait a minute. I done heard the bum shit before, but ain't nobody ever called me a poor excuse for a man. That's some new shit." He frowned.

"Well, I'm calling you that. Tell me how much money you got in your pocket right now." He took the blunt back from Stevo. The wind howled, and knocked the cherry from the Cigarillo. Makaroni hurried to pull it to his lips where he sucked and sucked to get the fire lit again.

"Yeah, well, you the only person that could call me that without me bussing yo ass. I don't give a fuck how broke I am. Mafuckas still gone respect me. That's just how that's finna go." Stevo clutched the handle of his pistol that was resting up against his lower abdomen. "Far as how much bread I got, I got about a hundred bucks. I sold a few bags of that Reggie." In Milwaukee when somebody referred to bud as Reggie it meant that it was the lowest form of potency. "Why? How much you got?"

Makaroni was busy trying to light the cigar again. He held it on his lips, and sparked the flame of his lighter over and over with no success. The wind was blowing too hard. After getting irritated he gave up, and held the half of blunt in his hand. "I got like five hundred. I been popping them bags too. But that still ain't no money. I need to cop me a whip. I need to help my mother with them bills that's coming at the end of the month. Plus, I'm tired of wearing the same old three pairs of pants. Now, I don't know what that fool Deacon on, but one thing is for sure. He is rich. He having that major white-collar paper. I'm trying to get my hands on some of that shit. You my right-hand mans, I'm trying to have you paid too. It's as simple as that."

Stevo took a long swallow from his bottle of Hennessey, and wiped his mouth with his gloved hand. His face was freezing cold. It was the shade of pink. His nose looked red. "You know I'm rolling with you. I ain't letting you go all the way down there without me. Never that." A shadow caught Stevo's eye. He perked up, and looked out of his backyard and into the alley. He could've sworn that he'd seen somebody's head peeking from the side of his garage. He pulled his gun halfway out of his pants. "Say, Makaroni, get up here on the porch beside me, nigga."

Makaroni was feeling the weed starting to kick in. He was stuck imagining how Kiana looked inside of her Prada jeans.

They made her ass look nice and round. He wondered how her pussy felt. She was little so he was sure that it was tight.

Stevo saw the shadows dance from the big light that was hung up on a pole in the back alley of his house. It was eight o'clock at night. He was sure he wasn't seeing things.

Makaroni snapped out of his trance and came up the steps. "Nigga, what's the matter with you?"

Stevo squinted. He searched harder. His nose felt as if it were frozen solid. "Dawg, let's go in the house. Come on." He turned around to push open the backdoor.

A masked Stacy hopped the back fence with a Mossberg pump in his hand. He was with two other Shooters. They hopped the fence, and stood beside him with guns in their hands, and white ski masks over their faces. Stacy rushed toward the back porch. He stopped after taking two steps, and fired, trying to take Stevo's head off.

Bloom!

The round slammed into the door just above Makaroni's head. He ducked, and forced his way into the house. Stevo moved so he could get into the door. As soon as he got past him, he pulled his pistol and got to bussing back to back. *Boom. Boom. Boom. Boom.*

Stacy held his ground. He bucked at Stevo. He was hoping that one or all of his shots would rip him to shreds. He hated him with a passion. He could never understand why Keaira had chosen him. He pulled the trigger again. The big Mossberg jumped in his hands, making him take a step back.

Both of his shooters started to spray their Uzis. It sounded as if a war movie was taking place right there in Stevo's backyard. Bullets hopped out of their weapons and landed in the snow, melting it all the way to the grass. Stevo let off three more shots and tried to slam the door. Stacy's bullet punched a massive hole through it. Stevo fell back. He landed on the steps, and took off running into the house.

Makaroni grabbed his .38 Special off of the table. It was next to a box of bullets. He had been getting ready to load it before Stevo asked him to step outside so they could smoke the blunt. Cassidy didn't mind the pair smoking, but she insisted that they did whatever they did outside of her home, and the back porch had been agreed upon as far enough for them to do what they did. Makaroni tried to open the cylinder to the .38 when he heard footsteps in the back hallway, followed by two Mossberg blasts that sent him falling backward over the glass table.

Stevo came running into the living room with his eyes as big as Frisbees. "Dawg, them bitch ass niggas behind me. We gotta get the fuck out of here!" He ran to the front door, and threw it open.

Makaroni jumped up, and ran behind him with the .38 Special in his hand. A bullet flew from the back of the house, and shattered the front room window. Makaroni stopped and aimed the empty gun at the trio then remembered that it was without bullets. He booked it outside. Stevo was already a half a block down.

Stacy watched as Makaroni ran out of the front door. He cleared the distance of the empty house as fast as he could. Jumped off of the porch and let off round after round at the pair, waiting to see if either one of them would fall. When neither did, he cursed under his breath. Seconds later his Hittas were standing behind him. He looked them over, and turned around. "Come on. We finna burn that nigga mama shit to the ground."

***

Stevo didn't stop running until he was ten blocks away from his house. His chest was killing him. He was so mad that he couldn't think straight. He slowed his sprint to a jog, and then to a walk. He wondered who it had been that tried to kill him. Second to that he was stuck wondering how he was going to explain the bullet holes to his parents.

Makaroni caught up a few paces later. He was breathing hard. "Damn, nigga. You left me." He started to coughing with his hands on his knees.

"Dawg, did you see who it was?" Stevo asked feeling like a pussy for having ran.

Makaroni shook his head. "N'all. All dem niggas had masks on. It could've been anybody." He stood up and started to walk down Lisbon Street with Stevo.

A Metro bus passed them packed with patrons. It drug close to the curb and spat up a bunch of dirty snow and slush with its tires. The mess landed on both men. It left them cold and smelly.

"Nigga, that's it!" Makaroni snapped. "I'm tired of this shit!"

Stevo lowered his head. "I know, dawg."

"N'all, fuck that, you don't know. If you knew, we would've been up in somethin'. Nigga, ain't you tired of the world shitting on you?"

Stevo nodded. "Yeah, but what can we do? We ain't got shit. We don't know nobody that do. And even if we did, mafuckas ain't trying to fuck with us." He waved Makaroni off, and started back to walking. His clothes felt heavy. The thighs on his pants were so wet that they were starting to freeze.

Makaroni stood there for a long time. He waited until Stevo got a nice distance before he took off running to catch up with him. When he did, he stepped into his face. "Nigga, you acting like a real bitch right now."

Stevo was shocked. He clenched his jaw, and bumped his chest against Makaroni's. "Fuck you say to me, nigga?"

Makaroni didn't hesitate. He knew that he had to handle Stevo rough in order for him to get motivated about anything. He pushed him out of his face. Then balled up his fists. He didn't know why he felt like fighting but he did. Tears threatened to come down his cheeks because of his frustrations with the world. He suppressed them. He needed to feel some physical pain. He knew that fuckin' around with Stevo, the man would deliver him just that.

Stevo loved Makaroni with all of his heart. He was the only family he felt he truly had at times, but he refused to allow for him to put his hands on him. He'd rather die first. He hopped into Makaroni's face and pressed his forehead to his. "Nigga, don't put yo mafuckin' hands on me again. You do, and we gon' have a serious ass problem."

Makaroni pushed him as hard as he could, then cracked him in the jaw hard. He didn't even know that he was about to actually hit Stevo until he did. Now he was forced to be all in.

Stevo stumbled back a few paces. He caught his balance, and sprung forward, swinging haymakers. The first blow caught Makaroni in the jaw. The second one busted his left eye. He picked him up and fell into the snow with him. They rolled around huffing and puffing. Makaroni wound up on top. He caught Stevo with two hard blows. Both to the face. Stevo's blood squirt across the snow. Cars continued to pass behind them. Lisbon Street was a busy one. Some of the commuters took pictures of the fighting pair with their phones, while others simply beeped their horns and kept it moving.

Stevo wiggled out of Makaroni's embrace, and jumped up with his guards up. "Aiight then, fuck nigga, let's get it."

Makaroni slowly came to his feet. He felt the blood seeping out of his eye. He neglected to wipe it away. His adrenalin was pumping too hard. His eye was stinging though. His jaw as well. The pain felt good to him. He smiled, and got ready to rush Stevo.

Stevo saw how Makaroni was bleeding, and his commonsense kicked in. He held up his hands. "Dawg, what the fuck are we doing?"

Makaroni swallowed his spit. He felt sick. He was tired of being a bum. Tired of being a low life. He hated how the world treated them. How the world saw them as less than human. He wanted better. He had to get rid of the pain in his heart. Tears fell down his cheeks. On the right side it was mixed with blood from his injury. He held his arms out. "Nigga, I love you. I'd rather feel the pain from my nigga than from this punk ass world. I can't take this shit no more, Stevo. I'm suicidal as a muthafucka." He dropped to his knees.

Stevo looked down at him. Then he checked their surroundings to make sure that there were no enemies trying to sneak up on them. His heart was heavy. He came to Makaroni and dropped to his knees beside him. Tears of exhaustion and hatred sailed down his face. He placed a hand on Makaroni's back. "Nigga, I'm sorry. I love you too. I swear to God that we ain't gon' always be bums. One day we gon' be rocking Jags and furs. Mafuckas gone look at us, and see the young Kings that we are. Mark those words."

Makaroni dripped blood into the snow. His wound was really leaking now. He felt lightheaded but he ignored it. "I wanna go see what's good with Deacon. If he can put us up on some serious change then we need to make that trip."

"I agree. Come on, let's get the fuck up out of here."

As they were standing up, a team of Fire Engines roared past loudly headed to Stevo's parents' home. The dark smoke from the blaze could be seen in the sky only a short distance away. Stevo's phone buzzed. He dug it out of his pocket, and read the face. It was a message from his father that read: *Come home quick. Our house is on fire. Hurry.* Stevo felt like he was about to pass out. He staggered backward.

"Bruh, what's the matter?" Makaroni asked.

Stevo replaced the phone in his pocket. "Our house on fire. Them fuck niggas must've lit it up. Come on." He took off running with Makaroni behind him.

***

When they got back to his house, it was fully engulfed. The firefighters had two trucks in the middle of the street trying their best to spray water on to the fire. The flames were violent. They shot up wildly, and showed very little resistance to the attacks of the firemen's hoses.

Cassidy pulled up to the corner of the street, parked her truck and took off running to the house. When she got two houses over from her own home she was stopped by the Fire Chief. "Ma'am, you have to stay back." She could feel the intense heat. The fire looked like it was about to spread to the neighbor's house on the left side of her home.

"But that's my house!" She shouted.

He shook his head. "Not anymore. I'm sorry."

Makaroni made it to her just as she was about to faint. He took her within his arms, and held her close. "It's okay, Cassidy. I got you. I already hollered at my mother. Y'all finna come and stay with us until you can get back on your feet."

Stevo watched from a distance. He didn't have the emotional capacity to be there for his mother. So, he stayed his distance. He watched his father Seth come over, and take his mother into his arms.

Makaroni eased away, and stood beside him. "Dawg, we really gotta take that trip now."

"I know. Make it happen, and I'm with you."

Chapter 7

Makaroni had been hitting Kiana up for two weeks straight. She had not answered any of his calls, or returned his messages. She'd also been missing from Facebook, and Instagram. He was praying that she was alright, and that she would get in touch with him soon. He had every intention on taking her up on her offer.

As he was standing in the kitchen, making a peanut butter and jelly sandwich, Montana came out of her bedroom with a mug on her face. "Damn, when they gon' leave up out of mama shit? This is a three-bedroom house. We ain't got enough room for them, and us too." She snapped.

Makaroni placed his finger to his lips. "Shush yo ass up. Damn. They been through a lot. Don't you got any compassion inside of you?" He asked, looking past her shoulder. Cassidy was coming out of the bathroom, and drying her hair, headed into his bedroom that he had allowed for her and Seth to sleep in.

"Nope. And as fucked up as life is, I don't know how you have any either." She grabbed his sandwich, and took a bite out of it. Walking out of the kitchen. "You coming to Ja-Michael birthday party this weekend?"

"What?" He started making another sandwich. His stomach growled. He had a taste for some real food, but peanut butter and jelly sandwiches were the only thing that they currently had in the house until Maisey got her food stamps in two days. "What party you talking about?"

"Our cousin JaMichael. He having a twenty fifth birthday bash down in Memphis. He celebrating his birthday, and the fact that he just got out of the Feds a week ago. Shit finna go down. I was told to invite you by him and his bitch."

Makaroni didn't even know who she was talking about. He had only heard the name mentioned a few times. "What kind of cousin is this nigga?"

"Uh, he is our second cousin. You don't really know him like that because you never spent none of your summers down in Memphis when mama wanted to send you. You too damn stubborn. But I went, and it's a whole different life down there. Way better than boring ass Milwaukee." She rolled her eyes, and took another bite off of her sandwich. She crossed her legs Indian style on the sofa. Closed her eyes and took another bite. Her short nightgown pulled backward to reveal that she wasn't wearing panties. Her naked sex lips were plump.

Makaroni found himself staring, and snapped out of his zone. "How the fuck you getting down there?"

"I'm taking a rental. Jahliya gon' pay for it when I get down there. You're welcome to come too. You can bring Stevo thirsty ass too."

Stevo stepped into the room upon the mentioning of his name. "Ain't shit thirsty about me." He looked right up her gown and saw that she was showing off her pussy for all to see. He wondered if Makaroni had caught a glimpse of it. Then again he figured that it was impossible not to see it from where they were standing. His dick began to telescope. "What you talking about anyway?" His eyes stayed on her pussy lips.

"My cousin having a birthday bash in Memphis this weekend. I was just telling Mack about it. I told him that we were invited, and that he could bring you too. That's it, that's all." She ate the last bite of her sandwich. Her knees remained spaced apart.

Stevo's piece was jumping up and down like crazy. He needed to find a way to get Makaroni out of the room so he could make his move on Montana. She was so thick and enticing to him. She had never given him the pussy, but he wanted to change all of that. "Bruh, why don't you go get dressed so we can hit up the Avenue. Try to get some paper and whatnot."

"Is the shower free now?" Makaroni inquired.

"Yeah, you good. My mother just came out of there."

"Aiight, cool. Montana, tell JaMichael we'll be there. We just gotta get some ends before we head that way."

"Sounds good. Y'all bet not embarrass me though!" She shouted at them.

Makaroni waved her off. "Shorty, shut yo ass up." He stepped into the hallway, came outside of his bedroom door and knocked on it.

"Who is it?" Cassidy asked as she put lotion on to her light caramel legs.

"It's me, Cassidy. I just need to grab me a fit so I can get in the shower."

"It's cool, baby, come in."

Makaroni opened the door. The first thing he saw was Cassidy wrapped in a big white terry cloth towel. Her thick thighs were on display. She squirt lotion into her hands, and rubbed them all over the right one. Makaroni felt like he couldn't breathe. He stepped inside, and closed the door behind him. "Where is Seth?"

She continued to rub the lotion into her blemish-less skin. "He left for work early this morning."

"Aw." Makaroni continued to drink in her sexy legs. She was well put together. He even took the time to peep her toes which were freshly painted, and French tipped.

"I thought you came in here to look for somethin' to wear." She teased.

Makaroni blushed. "Aw, yeah." He walked over to his dresser, and pulled on the old drawer. There was a mirror on top of it. From that angle he could see right up her towel, before it faded to darkness. She had her thighs closed just a bit too tight. All it would've taken was for her to open them a little bit, and he would've been able to see everything that she was working with down below. He shook from the anticipation.

Cassidy opened her thighs, and rubbed lotion on the inner portion of them. Unbeknownst to herself she was showing her son's best friend her sex.

Makaroni was rock hard by this point. All pretenses of not spying on her through the mirror were out the window. He gripped his piece, and squeezed it. "Mmm."

Cassidy looked up at him. "Makaroni, you got a thing for me, don't you?" Her hand slipped between her thighs, and stroked her pussy. She toyed with the lips until there was dew on them.

He turned around to face her. His piece poked out against his pajama pants. "On some real ish, Cassidy?"

She nodded. "Yeah, son."

He nodded. "I'm feening for yo fine ass."

She laughed, and covered her mouth. She could smell the scent of her freshly washed pussy on her digits. "Come here."

Makaroni felt like he was about to drop to the floor, his knees were so weak. "You for real?"

She opened her thighs wide. Her pussy was on full display. Fat. The lips were already engorged. "I got a thang for you too, son."

***

Stevo pushed Montana into the pantry, and bent her over. He yanked up her gown. Searched between her thighs until he found her box. Then he was fingering her at full speed. "Bitch, you like showing off this lil' pussy, don't you?" He hissed.

Montana spaced her feet. "Unn. Unn. Shut up. Get off of me." She tried to fight away from him.

Stevo thrust her further up against the lower shelf. Her forehead rested against a five-pound bag of sugar. He sped up his fingering. "You like this shit, bitch. Don't you? You like a mafucka playing with this pussy. That's why you was showing it off to me and Makaroni."

She yelped, and arched her back. "Unnnn, shut up. Shut up. Fuck." She shivered and came hard. Her knees grew weak.

Stevo picked her up, and got behind her. As much respect as he had for Makaroni he knew that Montana was a hoe. She had always been a tease. Hot blooded none the less, but a tease. Now that he had her nice and wet, he thought that it would be beneficial for him to drive her crazy. He pulled out his dick, and ran it up and down her pussy's groove. His head found her opening. He pushed inside her and got to fucking her as hard as he could. Her cat was as tight as a closed fist, and wet as a swimming pool.

"Aw fuck." She acted like she wanted to get away from him.

"Admit it, bitch." Stevo whispered. He yanked her back to him and got to ramming deep.

"Admit what? Aw. Aw. Aw. Fuck!"

"Admit. That. You. Was. Showing. Makaroni. Dat. Pussy. Too."

The thought of what Stevo was saying was so wrong that it seemed to strike a chord with her clitoris. She knew that her gown was short. She figured that Makaroni could see up it, but she almost dared him to look. She didn't know if he did or not and she didn't care. She felt Stevo slide so deep in her that it felt like the head of his piece was touching her navel.

Stevo slammed her ass hard. "Admit it!"

She came again. "No!"

Stevo threw her to the floor. He got between her thighs, and forced her into a ball. "Bitch, I'm Makaroni. This what I'd be doing to this fat ass pussy everyday living in a house with you. This what he told me he done dreamed about doing a hundred times." Stevo lied. He slid back in and got to fuckin' her hard. "I'm Makaroni."

Montana came back to back imagining that Makaroni was fucking her. As kids they had played Doctor, and husband and wife as most kids. Explored each other's bodies but it had always been innocent. Now that Stevo was putting these images in her head, it was driving her crazy. She stayed in the fantasy land along with him. Her clit throbbing worse than it ever had before.

Stevo leaned down, and sucked on her neck. "You belong to me, sis." He proceeded to pound her as hard as he could. Her juices made a puddle beneath them.

***

Cassidy fell to her knees. She took a hold of Makaroni's piece, stroked it up and down licking her juicy lips. "Mack, you always been like my baby. It's crazy how much you always try to protect me. I wish that Stevo was just like you." She looked into his eyes, before sliding him into her mouth.

Makaroni felt her heat. He steadied himself. He couldn't believe that fine ass Cassidy was sucking his dick. It felt so good. Her lips were tight. Trained, and wet. He felt a twinge of guilt because of her being Stevo's mother. Then her towel fell to reveal her gorgeous forty-year-old body. Her light caramel breasts were round. They jiggled while she sucked. The nipples were erect. Both stood at attention. The areolas covered a nice portion of each mound.

She sucked loudly. Groaning, and moaning. She popped him out. "Why do you always try to protect me, Makaroni?"

Makaroni squinted down at her. "'Cause, you like my mama too. I care about you."

Cassidy grabbed his dick aggressively, she sucked him back into her mouth and speared her face in his lap at full speed. She wanted to taste his cum. She needed to. There was something inside of her that craved him.

Makaroni shivered. He grabbed a handful of her hair. He humped her mouth faster and faster. "I'm finna cum, ma. I'm finna cum."

She sucked harder. She popped him out of her mouth, and pumped him swiftly. "Cum fa mama, baby. Please. Let me see it."

Makaroni grabbed her head, and stuck his piece back into her lips, then he was cuming hard. Humping. Grunting. His eyes wide open so he could watch Cassidy slurping him up.

***

Stevo came all over Montana's belly. He left big globs everywhere. He stood up, and looked down on her. Her thick thighs were wide open. "Damn, you got some good ass pussy."

Montana sat up. She pulled down her gown. His nut soaked into the material. She stood up. It felt like her pussy had been dug out. "Why you say all that sick shit about my brother? That threw me off." She lied. She was now embarrassed. She didn't want Stevo to know that his scenario her got her off.

Stevo laughed. He rubbed her pussy under her gown. It was still leaking. "Man, I ain't gon' tell him nothing, or nobody else. The only reason I told you about his dreams is because I know you ain't gon' say nothing either."

"Ain't nothing to say. That shit sick. I don't get down like that." She scrunched her face.

Stevo grabbed a hold of her, and slammed her against the wall. "Bitch, I don't care. Me and Makaroni talk about how bad you is all the time. He know you thick. That nigga got eyes just like I do. One day you gone give him some of this pussy. Watch." He slid two fingers into her, and sucked on her neck.

Montana started to shake. "Get off of me, Stevo. I need to go shower."

He laughed. He rubbed his fingers over her lips, then kissed her. "Yeah, you go do that then. With yo thick ass." He kissed the side of her face, and left her stuck standing in the pantry.

Montana waited for him to leave. Then she pulled the pantry door closed. Fell on her back, and rubbed her cat until she came whimpering Makaroni's name. She hated herself but couldn't help it.

***

Stevo knocked on Makaroni's bedroom door. "Mama, Makaroni in there?"

Makaroni took his face from between her thighs. She had just opened them so he could get a taste of her charms. Makaroni jumped up, and grabbed a bunch of clothes from his dresser. "Yeah, here I come, bruh." He hollered with his heart pounding in his chest.

Cassidy hurried and got dressed. She opened the bedroom window, then sprayed some of her perfume. Fanning her hand through the air. "Boy, go out there before he come in here." She whispered.

Makaroni nodded. He grabbed his clothes, and opened the door. Stevo stood in the hallway shaking his lighter up and down with a blunt in his mouth. "Gimme a minute to take a quick shower. I'll be right out."

Stevo waved him off. "Yeah, aiight. Hurry up so we can go get some pocket change. I got a lick for us to hit." He mugged his mother from the hallway. Then closed the door as she waved to him. He walked back into the living room shaking his head. He would never forgive her for what she'd done. It would take him a lifetime, and it wasn't because of what had taken place with Makaroni; he had no idea about that.

Ghost

Chapter 8

"Aiight, check this out. We at this fat bitch named Pam crib. She popping them nickel bags of Boy. Word on the street is that she be seeing every bit of three gees a day. It's about twelve o'clock right now. That mean her fat ass been in there selling that shit all day long." Stevo glanced up to her house from inside of his driver's seat. They were parked two houses down, and directly down the block.

"Nigga, so we supposed to go up there and rob some female for her lil' paper? You got me fucked up. I ain't doing that shit." Makaroni snapped with disgust in his voice.

"Who gives a fuck if she's a female, nigga? Money ain't got no mafuckin gender. When you spend that shit, they don't ask you if yo scratch is male or female. Fuck type of shit is you on?"

Makaroni mugged him. "Nigga, I'm not finna go up there and rob no female. That shit just seem weak to me. It's a thousand Dope Boys in this city. We can stay up all night hitting each one of they ass. I ain't finna rob no bitch, though, unless she's collateral damage. That's just that."

"Then where you want me to drop yo ass off at then?" Stevo was done already. He wasn't about to go through all of that bullshit with Makaroni. He was leaking. He knew that Pam had a few gees stashed in her crib, and he had to have it. He didn't care if she was a female or not.

"What?"

"You heard me. Where I'm finna drop yo nice ass off at?"

Makaroni mugged him with mounting anger. "Nigga, you ain't gotta drop me off nowhere. Gone in there and handle yo business. I'll be right here when you come out."

Stevo pulled out his .9 millimeter that he'd gotten from the first Dope Boy's robbery, and cocked it. "Bet, nigga. I'll be

71

back in a few minutes." He opened the door to the car. He looked out into the block both ways before he stepped out into the night. He closed the door and jogged to the side of Pam's house after hopping the fence to her yard. He stopped and listened for any sounds. After hearing none, he did a perimeter check of the house. When he got back to the front of it, he started to wonder how he was going to get Pam to open the door for him. He'd been told that she didn't serve any dope after eleven at night. That angered him. He stood there for a second, then looked out at Pam's money green 2020 Lexus. He smiled. He knew how he was going to get her to open the door. He looked both ways once again. Then he ran to her car and kicked it as hard as he could. The alarm started to blare. He hopped over her porch's banister, and waited on the side of the house breathing hard.

Makaroni watched from the passenger's seat. He felt that Stevo had to be out of his mind. He looked at his friend as he stood with his back against the wall of Pam's house breathing as if he was seconds away from having an asthma attack. Makaroni saw that his inhaler sat there on the driver's seat. He hoped that Stevo didn't actually break out into a full-fledged attack. That would have been disastrous.

Stevo wheezed. He swallowed his spit, and tried to lay as close to the house as he could. He saw the curtain pull back from the corners of his eyes. His adrenalin began to pump.

Pam tried over and over again to shut the alarm off. Her key chain remote wasn't working. She grabbed her .380 pistol from the table of her front room. Cocked it, and headed toward the front door. First, she peeked out the window again to make sure that she couldn't see anybody. After confirming it, she unlocked the front door, and stepped on to the porch. With her right hand she clicked the remote to try to disable her alarm.

After three presses it finally clicked off. She looked her whip over, and got ready to ease back into the house.

Stevo slid from the wall and smacked her in the side of the face with his .9 millimeter. She stumbled against the railing. Blood poured down the side of her head immediately. She felt dizzy. Stevo grabbed her, and smacked the .380 out of her hand. It slid across the porch. He wrapped his arm around her neck, and pulled her back into the house. "Bitch, listen to me. I ain't wear no mask because I ain't playing no fuckin' games with you. You finna tell me where this money at, and I wanna know where the rest of that dope at. I come as a robber. Don't make me leave as a murderer. That's my game too."

Pam was wobbly. Her t-shirt was drenched with blood. "Yo, let me the fuck go, nigga. I ain't got shit for you in here, homeboy." She said with her East Coast accent.

Stevo was taken aback. "Aw, you think it's a mafuckin' game?" He tossed her to the floor expecting her to stay there.

Pam jumped up, and took off running through the house. She ran down the hallway, and opened the bathroom door. Two big pit bulls ran out of it, and headed toward Stevo barking loudly.

He stopped in his tracks, and aimed at first the one on the left. *Boom!* The bullet zipped into the animal's chest, and knocked a massive hole into its heart. The dog flipped onto its side after yelping loudly.

The second pit bull leaped, and locked on to his arm. Stevo placed the gun to its eardrum, and pulled the trigger knocking its doggy noodles all over the carpet. The pit bull flopped to the ground. Its paws were still running until it stopped altogether. The scent of brain and gunpowder emitted into the air.

Pam grabbed the assault rifle from under her bed. She slammed a hundred round clip into it, and pulled open the bedroom door. "Nigga, you thought it was sweet. Dis is Harlem, Dunn. Let's get it." *Boom! Boom! Boom! Boom!*

Bullets began to come at Stevo so fast that that he slipped, and twisted his ankle. He jumped back up, and ran full speed toward the wide-open front door. Bullets ate up the wall beside the door jamb. Sparks flew. He ran outside, and fell down the steps. Pam was on his ass. She stopped, and aimed. Then fired three rounds. *Boom! Boom! Boom!*

Stevo felt a hot slug pierce his left butt cheek. He screamed like a female. The weight of the bullet caused him to fall into the street. In doing so he hit his head on the side of a car hard. It knocked him out cold. Pam saw this. She smiled, and ran down to see her prey laying there vulnerable, ready to meet his Maker. She stood over him. "Dis is Harlem, nigga. Never forget that." She placed the barrel to the back of his head ready to pull the trigger.

Makaroni rolled the window down of Stevo's trapper. He aimed and finger fucked his .38 Special. *Boom! Boom! Boom! Boom!*

The first series of bullets caught Pam off guard. She felt hot slugs eating at her face. She drooped the assault rifle. She ran a few paces before things got blurry. Her brains oozed out of the holes on the side of her forehead. She staggered, and fell to her knees.

Makaroni ran up on her. "Bitch, you gon' pop my mans?" *Boom! Boom!* He knocked her face partially off. He jogged over to Stevo, and stuffed him in the back of the car. Then he grabbed the assault rifle from the street, and threw it on the floor of the backseat of the car, before getting behind the wheel and storming away.

***

"Aw-uh, shit. Fuck that. I can't take it. I can't take it. This shit hurt too bad!" Stevo hollered. He took another swallow of

74

his Hennessey, and chewed up two Percocet. He was laid out on his stomach on the floor of the basement.

Cassidy sighed in frustration. "Boy, you gotta be still. I almost had the damn thang." She announced.

"N'all, fuck that. You trying to hurt me on purpose." He countered. He didn't trust her. He felt that she was a rotten woman to say the least. She was the reason that he never hesitated to smoke a female. He never thought twice about putting his hands on one. She was the cause of it all.

"Son, can you talk some sense into him?" Cassidy asked Makaroni.

Makaroni knelt beside him. "Come on, bruh, let's do this shit together. I'm wit' you. You wanna take my hand while she grab that out of you?" He held it out to him.

Stevo slapped his hand away. "Nigga, if you don't get yo soft ass away from me; I know something. Fuck I look like?" He snapped.

Makaroni stood up. "Aiight den, man up. You acting like a real pussy right now. That's why I was trying to treat you like one." He looked down to Cassidy. "Excuse my language, ma."

She nodded in understanding. "It's cool, baby."

Stevo looked back at her. "Hurry yo ass up and get that out of me. Come on!" He yelled.

Cassidy tightened the gloves on her hands. She wiped away the blood from his left buttock. Then she was digging into it with her tool. "You okay, baby?"

Stevo clenched his teeth. The pain was the worst thing he ever felt in his life. He clenched his fists, and groaned as loud as he could without seeming like a chump. He was seconds away from pushing her off of him and telling them that the bullet was going to have to stay in him.

Cassidy gripped the bullet with her tool. She slowly pulled it out of his meat. It was caked with his blood, and bodily slime. She dropped it into a shot glass. It clinked. "There you go. Now just let me clean you up before I stitch everything together. You should feel good as new in a few weeks."

Stevo laid his face on his arms. "Man, shut the fuck up and do what you gotta do. Please, Cassidy." He squeezed his eyelids. Tears seeped out of them and sailed down his cheeks.

Cassidy felt like her heart was aching. It seemed as if no matter what she did for Stevo he never appreciated it, and he always hated her. For a mother to have a child that hated them was the most painful feeling in the world second to childbirth. She knew why he treated her the way he did.

Thirty minutes later Stevo was sewn up and good to go. Cassidy wiped him down again. Then she gathered up her medical contents, and stuffed them into her nursing bag. "Awright, I'll talk to y'all in the morning." She said this with her head down, and her heart heavy.

"Bye." Stevo retorted.

That felt like a dagger. "Okay, baby." She began to walk up the stairs.

Makaroni mugged his friend as he came to a stand wincing in pain. "Dawg, why the fuck you couldn't tell her thank you?"

"Thank you for what? Nigga, I'm her son. She only did what she was supposed to." He slowly made his way to the couch. He sat down on it sideways, exhaling loudly. "Fuck, that shit hurt. Mafuckas never know how much it hurt to get shot in the ass until it happens to them." He attempted a laugh.

Makaroni smacked his lips. "Nigga, yousa bitch for how you acting. You lucky God didn't let that bitch kill you tonight for how you treat your mother. You supposed to honor her. She left this basement crying."

"And? Fuck you want from me?" He quipped.

Makaroni pointed at him. "Bruh, just shut up. I'm finna go make sure she straight. You betta hope that she is or we finna have a major problem."

"Man, fuck both of y'all. I'm finna get some sleep. I'm tired as hell. I'll get at you in the morning."

Makaroni flipped him the middle finger. "Fuck you."

* * *

When he got upstairs, he found Cassidy sliding her purse over her shoulder. She had her car keys in hand. "Yo, ma, where you finna go?" He asked worried.

"I need to take a ride. My head is all screwed up. I just need to get out of here." She threw on her jacket, and opened the front door.

"You mind if I roll wit' you?" Makaroni asked already sliding his bomber jacket on.

She shook her head. "I mean, I kind of wanna be alone, but I guess I could use some company too. Come on, baby."

Every time she called him baby it drove him crazy. He allowed for her to lead the way. He glanced over his shoulder to see Montana step out of her room. "Where you finna go?"

"I'm finna roll wit' Cassidy right quick. We'll be back in a minute."

She nodded. "Aiight, but then me and you need to talk. Okay?"

"Cool."

Montana smiled weakly, and stepped back inside of her bedroom.

Ghost

Chapter 9

Cassidy pulled her car up to the overpass, and parked it inside of the parking lot. The sounds of her tires crunching on the snow was loud under the car. She threw the gear in park. She kept both the music, and heat playing. Sade's Sweetest Taboo serenaded the car. She eased her seat back, and ran her fingers through her hair.

Makaroni rested his hand on her thigh. "What's the natter, mama? Holler at me."

Cassidy flipped her hair out of her face. "Stevo hate me, and I don't know why. I thought he would grow out of his ill feelings toward me, but he hasn't. That's the worst feeling in all of the world."

Makaroni pulled her so that her head was resting on his shoulder. "I don't think he hate you. I think bruh just going through a lot in general. He don't know which way is up right now."

"Yeah, maybe. But he been this way for a long time. Sometimes it hurt me so bad that I don't know what to do." She sighed, and snuggled her head more comfortably on Makaroni's shoulder. "I love him, Mack, but I swear at times that I wish you were my son. I think I would trade y'all in a heartbeat." She laughed nervously. She knew she sounded ridiculous. But she didn't care. How could she when Stevo treated her like he did?

Makaroni kissed her forehead. "I'm lucky you ain't my mother." He rubbed her silky hair. The weight of her head on his shoulders somehow made him feel good. He could smell the sheen she used for her hair clear as day, along with her perfume. Cassidy smelled like a grown ass woman. He didn't know why he came to that conclusion, but it drove him crazy.

She picked her head up from his shoulder. "Excuse me? You making it seem like I'd be a terrible mother or somethin'." She was offended. "I don't know what Stevo has been telling you, but I did the best that I could with him and his sister, even though she wasn't my biological child."

Makaroni laughed. "N'all, ma, you tripping. I wasn't saying it like it was a bad thing. What I'm saying is that I'm so attracted to you. If you was my real mother we'd have to be on that Raised As A Goon type stuff. Mother and Son love all day every day. I don't think I could ever get enough of you." He admitted.

Cassidy had read all five books of Raised As A Goon by Ghost, and at the thought of some of the sex scenes inside of the books it drove her crazy. She brought her thighs together, and squeezed them. "Aw-uh, you really think you would been that crazy over me, even if I was your own mother?"

Makaroni had to keep it one hunnit. He imagined her walking around the house in the ways and night outfits that he'd seen her walk around Stevo's, and the images going through his brain made his piece start to jerk like crazy. "Hell yeah, I would've. I ain't never seen a female as fine as you before."

"Makaroni, I'm twice your age. It's a bunch of young girls that put me to shame." She said modestly.

"Yeah, right. But anyway, I'm here to talk about anything that you want. I just wanna be a shoulder for you to lean on."

Cassidy climbed across the console, and straddled him as best she could. The top of her head rested on the roof of the car. "What if I don't wanna talk no more tonight? Then what?" She leaned forward and sucked on his neck. Sade's Smooth Operator crooned out of the speakers at just the right volume.

He gripped her ass through her jeans. His fingers dug into the cheeks. They felt so soft. "I'm 'bout whatever you 'bout, mama."

Cassidy started to shake. "Don't call me that, baby. Not right now. Please. I'm too vulnerable for that."

Makaroni pulled her down, and slipped his face into the crux of her neck. Her perfume was louder. The heat of her skin seemed to call to him. He rested his cheek against her flesh first, and then his lips was upon her neck. He kissed ever so lightly. "I love you, mama. Stevo might be stubborn, but I ain't. I love how fine you is. I love how crazy you make me feel. I'm yo baby. And you mine." His tongue licked up and down the thick vein of her neck, before his teeth bit into her.

Cassidy moaned out loud. She tossed her head back, and humped forward. "I love you too, baby. I swear to God mama do."

Makaroni slipped his hands under her shirt. His fingers maneuvered until they were rubbing her hard nipples. He pulled on them. Then flipped her bra up altogether. He wished the interior lights were on. He would've loved to see them. Cassidy was so sexy to him. He sucked her left nipple while he tweaked her right. Then he was sucking the right one.

She humped faster and faster into him. "I wanna make love to you, baby. I don't care if we in this car. I need some of you." She climbed off of his lap and into the backseat. There, she unbuttoned her pants, pulled them down her thighs, and off. She could smell her own arousal. "Come on, son."

Makaroni ain't have to be told twice. He was already stripping as he climbed into the backseat. When he got back there, he fell between her legs. Her hot pussy was right up on his stomach. It felt damp, and soft. He positioned himself so that his dick head was laying on her sex lips.

She held his waist. "Mack, tell me that you love me. Tell me that I'm a good mother. Tell me that ain't no woman better than yo mama." She reached between their bodies, and slid his fat head between her lips.

Makaroni pushed into her wetness. He moaned. She was so hot, a shockingly tight. He couldn't believe that he was getting ready to fuck Stevo's mother.

Cassidy dug her nails into his waist. "Tell me, son."

"I love you, mama." He moved her hands and got to slow stroking her tight womb. She Kicked his neck. "You the best mama. Only you." He plunged deeper while she rubbed all over his back. "Ain't no woman. Better than. You, mama." He grunted, and sped up.

The windows slowly fogged with their passion. Their scent heavy in the car. Sade continued to assist their love making. Her voice eased Cassidy's tension. Her track gave Makaroni a rhythm to fuck to. It was a win-win situation.

"Ooo. Ooo. Ooo. Baby. Fuck me. Fuck me, baby... Ohhh my baby. Harder. Please." She opened her knees wider.

Makaroni had the car rocking on the wheels. He plunged deeper, and harder. Faster and faster. She got wetter. Her nails dug into his flesh. He sucked all over her neck. Then his tongue found its way into her ear.

Cassidy moaned at the top of her lungs. "You got mama cuming. I'm cuming, baby." She popped her cat into him, and came all over his positioning dick. Her walls pulled at his pole. Sucking like a mouth.

Makaroni's eyes rolled into the back of his head. He kept fucking. He leaned down and sucked all over her nipples. His hips continued to plow forward.

"I wanna feel your cum in me, baby. Please. Cum in mama. Cum in me. I know you'll love me then. Ohhh. Shit! It feel so good. Harder! Awwwww!"

Makaroni was fucking so fast that he could barely breathe. He forced her right knee to her chest and clapped into her middle. The feeling became so intense that he couldn't hold back any longer. He squeezed his eyelids together, and came back to back. Shooting jets into Cassidy.

She felt his passions, and it released another orgasm to rock through her womb. She sucked on his shoulder, and screamed against it. Sweat slid down the side of her face. She pulled him down on top of her. "I love you, baby. I love you so, so much. Do you hear me?"

Makaroni was exhausted. His piece continued to jump inside of her. "I hear you, ma. I love you too." He still couldn't believe that he had fucked Stevo's mother. What was worse than that was how good it felt. He knew he was going to have a hard time looking him in the eye.

***

"Stevo. Stevo. Wake up. Yo ratchet ass baby mama out front about to get her ass whipped of she don't gone with all of that bullshit." Montana reported, nudging him enough to jar him awake.

Stevo's eyes slowly opened. They were crossed at first. Then he came to his senses. "Fuck is she out there doing?" He asked getting up. He must've forgotten that he had been shot. His ass cheek bumped the couch. He tensed in pain, and shot up.

Montana jumped back with her eyes wide open. "I don't know what her issue is. That's yo broad. But I'ma tell you like this; this ain't even y'all house to be having drama popping off here. You need to get that bitch under control. Straight up."

Stevo snatched Montana to him, and kissed her on the lips. "Bitch, quit all that tough shit. You ain't 'bout that life." He pushed her away from him. She landed on the couch stuck.

When he got upstairs, he could Keaira blowing the horn to her car over and over again. He was thankful that Maisey worked third shift or else he was sure she would've had a fit. He stepped out on to the porch, and threw his arms up. "Fuck is up?" He hollered.

Keaira jumped out of her mother's car, and made a beeline for the porch. "Where the fuck you been at? Huh?"

Stevo was groggy. He didn't feel like he had the patience to deal with a stuck up, disrespectful Keaira. His ass cheek was hurting him. "Look, bitch, if you think you finna come over here with that bullshit you got another thing coming. Get yo punk ass in the car and get the fuck out of here."

She gasped in shock. "Oh, nigga. Dat's how you think you finna talk to me after how you left me stranded a few days ago? You ain't even called to see if I made it home safely, or if I was okay. You got some fuckin' nerve."

"Man, bye, bitch. Ain't nobody got time for this." He could feel blood running down his thigh.

"Did you know that your son had a fever? Huh? Did you know that I was in the hospital with him for two days straight because of his severe ear infections? Did you?" She snapped.

"N'all, I didn't know that. But what you want me to do about that shit now? I mean he aiight now, ain't he?" Though Stevo sounded like an asshole he really did care about the status of his son.

"You know what? Since you acting like a dick, it ain't even your concern. I feel like a fool for coming over here." She made her way back to the car. That's when Stevo saw a male figure move in the passenger's seat.

He jumped off of the porch and made haste to the passenger's side. He pulled open the door. The dude nearly fell out. "Nigga, who the fuck is you?"

Keaira cursed under her breath. "Don't worry about who he is. Who he is ain't got shit to do with you."

"Oh really?" Stevo pulled his .9 millimeter out of his waist, and cocked it. "Nigga, I'm gone ask you one more time, who is you?"

The dude threw his hands up. "Look, bruh, I met shorty at a club. We just been chilling for a few days. I ain't got nothing against you."

"Nigga, you seen my son?" Stevo asked.

"Stevo, close the fuckin' door. We need to get out of here."

"Bitch, shut up." He pointed the gun at her. "Nigga, answer my mafuckin' question. You been around my son?"

He nodded. "Yeah. I only held him once. She gave him to me. I didn't hurt him or none of that. I would never hurt a kid."

Stevo mugged Keaira. "Yeah, bitch. This what we on right now? Huh?"

She crossed her arms as snow began to fall from the sky. "Here we go with this shit."

Stevo looked back into the light skinned man's face. "Check this out, homie. Sometimes bitches put you in a fucked up position." He cocked back the gun, and slammed it forward into the man's face, smashing five of his teeth in. The man spit out the broken teeth, along with blood and mucus. He stood up out of the car, holding his mouth.

"Stevo, what are you doing?" Keaira screamed.

"Bitch, shut up." He aimed the gun at her for the second time. "Get yo punk ass in the car. Now. You too."

She got behind the steering wheel, and slammed her door. She felt sick on the stomach. She was wishing that she had never came to see Stevo, especially with another man being present. She should've known that he was going to snap.

Stevo slipped into the backseat, and pressed the gun to the back of the man's head. "Bitch, drive over to the can place on Thirty Second and Auer. Now!" He hollered.

Keaira stepped on the gas. She was shaking like crazy. "Look, Stevo, I'm sorry. I should've never brought another man around our son. I was wrong for that, but he didn't know what he was walking into."

"Bitch, that's yo fault." Stevo winced in pain as his gunshot wound began to throb like never before. He grit his teeth. His left shoe was full of blood.

Keaira pulled in back of the can place. It was located right next to the railroad tracks. There weren't any streetlights present. It looked dark, and scary. "Why are we coming here?" She asked in a shaky voice.

Stevo snapped and wrapped his arm around the dude's throat. He placed the gun to his temple. "Get yo ass out the car. Come on. Bitch, you come too." He ordered.

The dude followed his directives. "Please, man. I'll give you anything."

"Get on yo knees, bitch." He ordered him. "Keaira, come here." He pulled the .38 Special out of his waistband now and pointed it at Keaira.

She ran around until she was standing beside him. "What, Stevo? What are you finna do?" She cried.

"N'all, bitch. You made this mess. It's what you're finna do." He pulled her to him while balancing the gun in his right hand. He got behind her, and bit into her shoulder. He cocked the .38. "Kill his bitch ass. Now. Pull the trigger."

Keaira tried to break away from him. "No!"

He wrapped his arm around her neck. "Bitch, I promise if you don't then I'm finna kill you right here tonight. Now fuck this nigga. Pull the trigger."

"Please, man." The dude begged. Blood ran down his neck. He could feel the rocks cutting into his knees.

"Do it, Keaira." He stepped back from her, and aimed his .9 millimeter at her. "Bitch, it's either him or you. Far as I'm concerned, it can be both of y'all. You got three seconds."

Keaira was shaking so bad that she had to pee. She squeezed out a trickle. She heard Stevo count from one to two. "I'm sorry, God. Please forgive me."

The dude started to get up. "No, no. Please." Before he could make it to his feet, Keaira fired a lethal round. It zipped from her gun and smashed into his forehead, knocking two sections of his brain out the back of his skull. His noodles leaked down his neck. He was dead before he fell face-first.

Stevo came and stood over him. "Good shot, baby. Now next time you'll know better. Let's go."

Keaira dropped the gun and fell to her knees screaming into her hands. She couldn't believe that she had killed some-body. She couldn't believe that she was a murderer. She was sure that she was going to hell. She could hear Stevo in the background busting up laughing with no remorse.

Ghost

Chapter 10

"Bruh, you telling me that we actually finna go down here broke as hell? Do that make any sense to you?" Stevo asked Makaroni. He adjusted the .9 millimeter on his waist. They were fifteen miles away from Memphis. He had never been before. The fact that it was the first time and he was going broke made him feel like scum.

"Well, we tried to do shit yo way but all that cost me was a murder, and you a slug to the ass." Makaroni snickered.

Stevo elbowed him. "Fuck you, nigga." He twisted the cap off of his Hennessey, and began to drink from the bottle until he could feel the warm feeling in his belly.

"N'all, but Montana already hollered at my cousin n'em. She told them that we fucked up right now. JaMichael having that stupid gwop, him and Jahliya. Montana say they gon' put us up on some major money. All we gotta do is come down here. So chill, nigga. Besides, after what you did to Keaira's nigga you need to be out of Milwaukee for a minute."

"It wasn't her nigga, first of all. Second of all, I ain't do shit to him. She pulled the trigger and knocked his shit loose. I was an innocent bystander." He took another swallow from his bottle.

Makaroni looked over at him like he was a damn fool. "That's your story, huh?"

"Yep, and I'm sticking to it like lint on a suede suit." He closed his eyes, and laid his dome back on the headrest. "What's up with that Kiana bitch? I thought we was supposed to be meeting up with her Pops down in Miami. What? That bitch changed her mind or something?"

Makaroni shrugged. "You know how these hoez get down. If it ain't one thing it's another. She still ain't hit me up, and her social media pages been nonexistent. I don't know what's good, but I ain't about to dwell on it."

"Yeah, fuck her then. We'll figure shit out, bruh. We always do." He balled his hand into a fist.

Makaroni bumped it with his own. "Look, Stevo, when we get down here, we gon' need to stick together. It's finna be plenty of bad bitches that a get a mafucka lost. Don't come up missing, nigga. When you move, I move. It's as simple as that. Cool?"

Stevo nodded. "On some real shit, I ain't even thinking about no pussy right now. When I left Keaira, that bitch was still breaking down over popping dude ass, and that was three weeks ago. She ain't been to work either. That mean she gone have to get more government assistance. The more assistance she get, the higher they raise my child support. That mean that even if I wanted to get a job, it'll be pointless because they would take everything. But on the flipside, if I don't start paying that shit, them people gone come looking for me to lock me up. It just seem like if it ain't one thing that it's another."

"How much you owe so far?" Makaroni wanted to know. He was glad that he didn't have any children. He knew that they cost an arm and a leg. He did want a family one day, but he wanted it to come down the line when he had himself together, and was financially stable.

"I owe about five thousand so far."

"Five gees. What?" Makaroni was in disbelief. "How much time they make you do in prison for that amount?"

"Nigga, they ain't finna make me do no time in prison because I ain't going. They gon' have to kill me before anything happen like that." He was getting riled up. His eyes were turned into slits. His chest rose and fell over and over. Stevo had only previously served eight months in the House of Corrections, which in Milwaukee was like a prison sponsored by the county. He felt like it was the worst time of his life. Every day he woke up hoping to die because of the ill and unfair treatment by the police there. The living conditions were also terrible. He was forced to sleep on bunkbeds around a bunch of disgusting men with terrible hygiene practices, and disrespectful natures. Within the eight months he'd gotten into fifteen fights, and stabbed eight people. It was a warzone; that was the only part of the set up that he liked.

"Yeah, I get all that, but do you know if there really is a certain amount of time that they make people serve for that amount of money that is owed?"

He shrugged. "Don't know, and I don't care. I ain't paying them shit. I take care of mine. Always have, and I always will." He grabbed a blunt out of the ashtray, and sparked it. They were rolling past a marsh. The trees were already looking funny to him. It reminded him of every slave movie he had already seen. "Dawg, ain't they real racist in Tennessee?"

"I think they racist everywhere, bro. Shid, it can't be no worse than Wisconsin."

Stevo watched them roll past the sign that told them they were entering into Memphis. "I know one thing is for sure, we gotta ditch this hot ass whip. It's be fucked up if we got all the way down here, and then was pulled over for riding in a car that was stolen. You feel me?"

"Hell yeah, I do. All we gotta do is roll over here to this burger joint in Orange Mound. I'm texting Montana right now letting her know that we're here." Makaroni kept driving with his left hand, while his right thumb went to work. Every now and then he would look from the road to his phone, then back again.

"Nigga, if she already here then why the fuck didn't we roll down wit' her? We coming all the way from Wisconsin in a hot ass Steamer." In the Midwest, Steamer was a street way of saying stolen car.

"'Cause she flew down a few days ago. My cousin Jahliya sent for her. Anyway, it's too late for that now, we're already here. Besides, if yo shit didn't break down before we even got off of my block, we wouldn't have had to steal a fuckin' car. You ever think about that?" Makaroni shot back at him.

"Dat's why I'm hoping yo people about to put us up on somethin'. Straight up." He leaned back, and closed his eyes again. "Wake me up when we get there."

***

Fifteen minutes later Makaroni pulled up to Nita's House of Hamburgers right outside of The Orange Mound. It was a small restaurant that looked like a burgundy barn. Makaroni parked the car, and turned off the ignition. The gas tank was nearly empty. He had fifty dollars to his name, and a quarter ounce of Reggie. The sun was just starting to set. He yawned and covered his mouth with his hand. "Man, wake yo ass up. If I can't sleep then you can't either."

Stevo slowly opened his eyes. "Damn, nigga, I'm tired as hell. Fuckin' wit' Keaira, I been up for the last three days straight praying to God that she didn't flip out and go to the police. You already know how that shit go." He stretched his arms out until his fists brushed up against the ceiling. His mouth opened wide.

Makaroni wanted to close his eyes for a second but he knew that wouldn't be wise. He didn't know much about Memphis, but he'd heard that the boys down there were about that action. He needed to stay alert to ensure that they didn't wind up on the receiving end of some bullshit.

A bum with an old newspaper in his right hand and a bottle of Windex that he'd stolen from the gas station bathroom walked right up to the car and got on top of it. He sprayed the window, and started to cleaning it with the newspaper.

Makaroni waved him off. "Man, gone. We don't need that shit."

Stevo mugged him. He looked around to see how many people were watching. He wanted to get out of the car and kick his as real fast. "Dawg ,would you feel some type of way if I popped dude bitch ass?" He continued to scan the parking lot. There were a few other cars parked in the lot. A van, and a sports car. Across the street from them was a liquor store that looked packed. Stevo didn't care though. He felt that didn't anybody in Memphis know them. He could pop the bum, and nobody would be the wiser.

"Nigga, we ain't down here for that dumb ass shit. Besides, the mafucka probably just hungry." He grabbed the bag of left-over cheeseburgers from McDonald's. Opened the door to his car, and stepped out. "Say, homie, we ain't got no money, but you can have these cheeseburgers."

The bum slowly slid off of the car, and staggered on his feet. He walked up to Makaroni with the bottle of Windex in his hand. "Thank you, Mane." He set the newspaper on the hood, and reached for the bag with his left hand.

Makaroni handed the bag to him. "Enjoy that."

"Oh, I will. Thank you." He took the bag, and flung it to the ground. Then upped a .40 Glock. "Nigga, break yo self. You too." He said to Stevo.

Makaroni put his hands into the air. "Ain't this a bitch?"

"You muthafuckin' right it is." He flung him over the hood of his car. Two of his buddies came running out of the alley beside the restaurant with guns in their hands. They were at Stevo's window before he could even grasp what they had gotten themselves into.

"Aiight, man." Stevo kept his hands up.

The passenger's door was pulled open. He was yanked out, and forced to the ground. He felt his pockets being cut off of him while a shotgun was pressed to his cheek. They took off his shoes and socks. Next came his pants.

Makaroni was already stripped to the underwear. After he was a clothing article from being naked, the bums jumped in the stolen Buick and stormed away. "Dat's what y'all bitch ass get for loafing." The original bum hollered.

Stevo waited until they pulled out of the parking lot before he jumped up furious. "You gotta be kidding me."

Makaroni got up. He felt like a damn fool. Once again, his heart had gotten the better of him. He tried to do the right thing only to be rewarded by the wrong thing. He wondered why life was such a bitch.

Stevo walked up to him. "Nigga, you need to turn dis mafucka cold. You see what the fuck just happened? Huh? Do you?" He snapped.

Makaroni couldn't meet his eyes. He looked past his shoulders. He damn near shit himself when he saw the same Buick rolling back into the parking lot. He tapped Stevo on the shoulder. "Dawg, them bitch ass niggas coming back. What the fuck are they on?"

Stevo was so mad that he didn't care to retreat. Instead of running away he walked toward the car with his arms out. "Fuck y'all wanna do? Huh? What y'all wanna do?"

The Buick swerved and parked. The first bum got out of the passenger's seat with two guns in his hand. Half of his face was covered by a mask now. His three goons stood behind him.

Makaroni fell the ground shaking as if it were about to be an earthquake. He mugged the culprits, and then searched for where the vibrations were coming from. He looked over to Stevo. He could see him baling and unballing his fists.

Montana rounded the corner in an all-black on black Hummer. It was her first time driving it on the open road, but she felt like she had it mastered. Her cousin Jahliya sat in the passenger's seat with a Draco on her lap. She wore pink Prada gloves that matched her Prada boots. Montana pulled up on Makaroni and Stevo with a big smile on her face. She lowered the tinted driver's window. "What's good, niggas?"

Stevo never took his eyes off of the dudes that had just robbed him. He wanted to take their lives. The hatred inside of him started to make his nose bleed.

Montana jumped out of the Hummer, and ran around to open Jahliya's door. Jahliya stepped out outfitted in a Prada pants suit. She grabbed both Makaroni's and Stevo's clothes, and stepped up to Makaroni. "Huh lil' cuz. Next time, don't make it so easy for a mafucka to get yo ass."

Makaroni looked into her fine light brown face. She had dimples in each cheek, yet he could see the killer in her eyes. She stood five feet four inches tall. Weighed a hundred and thirty pounds. Her hair fell just below her shoulders, curly. She smelled like money. Her fragrance was intoxicating to him. He took his clothes from her, and threw Stevo his. "So you had this fuck shit did to us?"

She shook her head. "I ain't do shit. Dese my Potnas doe. They work this strip. If a mafucka get caught loafing over here, they got the go ahead to lay they ass down. They still gotta report that shit to me though. Just so happened that they seen them Wisconsin plates and knew it was finna be sweet. So, they moved on y'all." She smiled at them. "I saw them down yonder with those plates and I knew they had to just jacked y'all for y'all shit. Welcome to Memphis." She stepped up to Makaroni to give him a hug.

Makaroni hugged her tight. He took a step back and kissed her cheek. "I'ma need them guns back, and my lil' paper."

She laughed. "I'm already knowing. It's in the whip already. Let's ride out."

Makaroni noticed that Stevo was still mugging the foursome that robbed them. He had hatred on his heart. "Bruh, let's roll. Let that shit go."

Stevo continued to mug them. "Which one of you niggas put that shotgun to my cheek?"

A masked robber stepped forward. "Dat be me, Mane. Wasn't nothing personal. Just handling our business. Dat's what it is down here."

"Nigga, let me see yo face. I mean, I can let that shit go." He lied. "But I at least wanna see the face of the nigga who treated me like a bitch."

The masked robber laughed. "Dat ain't how dat work, Playboy. Now gone. Consider yo self saved by the Queen of the South." He turned and walked away. His crew of robbers disappeared into the darkness behind the restaurant, waiting for their next victim to pull up.

Stevo stared in their direction until he could bring himself to get dressed. Then he jumped in the Hummer beside Makaroni with his temper boiling. Before he left Memphis, he vowed to find out just who it was that placed the barrel to his cheek. He wouldn't be able to sleep right until he sent that robber to the Reaper.

Chapter 11

Makaroni couldn't believe his eyes as he stepped into the two-story mansion that was supposed to be his cousin Jahliya's. He never met a Boss Bitch before, and couldn't for the life of him understand how Montana had been able to keep Jahliya a secret for as long as she had. The mansion was all white on the outside, and the inside was more of the same. It looked clean. Jahliya had maids that rotated work assignments on all three shifts. She was a stickler about keeping the place clean. It smelled just as clean as it looked.

Along the walls were huge paintings of famous, powerful women like Michelle Obama, Condoleezza Rice, Shirley Chisolm, and Shondra Rimes. Her chandeliers sparkled bright. Her couches were white leather. She had marble counters and floors. Her staircase leading up to the second story was in a zigzag with white carpeting.

There were two big glass doors that overlooked the pool out back. The pool was covered by a huge tarp. Further back from the ten-meter pool was a pool house that was equally decorated. Montana came up and put her arm around Makaroni's neck. "Nigga, this what a Boss Bitch look like. I'm finna fuck wit' Jahliya the long way. It's gon' be two Boss Bitches in the family. You can mark those words." She kissed his cheek.

Jahliya gave them the grand tour of the estate. When she finished they wound up in her meeting room. This room consisted of a long wooden table with chairs around it. At the very top was a pink throne. Jahliya took this seat, and rubbed the white fur of her female Yorke.

Makaroni sat at the table. A big bowl of Syracuse Orange was placed in front of him. Syracuse Orange was some of the best weed coming off of the east coast. He took ten big buds and rolled himself a blunt.

Stevo was trying to stuff his blunt with all of the weed that it could take. When he couldn't get anymore inside of his cigar, he dumped a handful in his shirt pocket. He didn't know who Jahliya was but she wasn't any kin to him, so she was taking advantage.

Montana mugged him. She couldn't believe how trifling he was acting. She felt that he was so embarrassing. She sat on Jahliya's right side, and crossed her thick thighs.

Jahliya crossed her fingers. "Do y'all know why I brought you in here today?" She asked both Makaroni and Stevo.

Makaroni blew a dark gray cloud into the air, and shook his head. "N'all, cuz. What do you have on your mind?"

Stevo took two pulls and was lifted. He broke out into a fit of coughs. His throat felt raw as if he had swallowed a potato peeler. He beat on his chest with his fist, and kept smoking.

"I brought you here, most specifically Makaroni, because I wanna help you get on your feet. My lil' cousin been telling me how much y'all are struggling up there in Wisconsin. I wanna change that as best I can. But I don't really do the handout type of shit. If you finna get it with me, you're going to have to put some work in. Y'all understand that?"

Makaroni nodded. "But of course."

Stevo's eyes were crossed. He was on his twentieth pull. He was so high that he could hear his heart beating inside of his chest. He swallowed his sparse spit, and squeezed his eyelids together. "Man, tell Shorty we ain't scared to get our hands dirty."

"Uh, you don't need to have him speak to me. If you are going to be working under me then you will address me with absolute respect. That's how this is going to go."

98

Stevo opened his eyes and looked up at Jahliya. She was so small. So fine to him. He couldn't imagine a female being in control or calling shots over him. Something about that just seemed unnatural to him. "Yeah, I hear you, Shorty."

Jahliya eyed him closely. "Excuse me? Shorty? Is that what you just called me?"

Stevo laughed. "Yeah, that's better than bitch, right?" He laughed.

Jahliya was in shock. She snapped her fingers. Two big beefy bodyguards rushed into the room. They stopped beside her. "Take him out of here. Maybe downstairs to the den. Do not let him leave that room until I tell you to. Got that?" She asked.

They nodded, and accosted Stevo. "Let's go, homie." The biggest of the two said. He stood six feet eight inches tall. He weighed three hundred pounds even, and was as solid as a mountain.

Stevo stood up. "Damn, I see Shorty ain't got no sense of humor."

The room was quiet while they led him out. Makaroni refused to make eye contact with him. He felt that Stevo was acting like an idiot. He was tired of his immaturity.

As soon as the door closed Jahliya stood up with the dog under her right arm. "Makaroni, you gon' have to check yo guy. He don't even know who I am. If I didn't have love for you, I would have his ass chopped into a hundred pieces. That ain't no joke either." She sat back on her throne.

Makaroni didn't wanna ruffle her feathers. He knew that females could be spiteful when they got angry. He loved Stevo. He didn't wanna see nothing happen to his brother. "Look, I apologize for his behavior. I'll make sure he get it together. You got my word on that."

"I'ma hold you to it. Awright, now let's get to business." She looked down the table at him. "Nigga, it's levels to this shit. Just because you're my family don't mean that you're going to surpass any level without putting that work in. So, based off of what I saw today with them lil' bum ass stick up boys stripping y'all like that, I need to make sure that you got that killa shit in you. Right now, I don't see it. You are judged in this game by your actions, and most importantly by the company you keep. Your circle is a reflection of you. That boy mirrors you. I mean, don't he?"

Makaroni was ten toes down for Stevo. He knew his homie was a killa. His actions painted a poor image of himself. "You know what? I'ma agree with you on that, cuz. But from here on out, you are going to see a completely different person than the one you met today. Extend myself as well as him that olive branch."

Jahliya stared at him in silence for a moment. "Notice I only got rid of his ass and not you. Consider that, and the fact that we are set to proceed, your olive branch."

Makaroni nodded. He took a few tokes of his blunt. "Okay, so what's the first level?"

Jahliya rubbed her dog. "Murder, cuz. I want you to get that blood on yo hands. I got a few rodents right here in Memphis that I need exterminated. You think you can handle that?"

Makaroni sat his blunt in the ashtray. He crossed his fingers and leaned forward. "You tell me how you want shit done and when. I'll show you what's really good. Me and my nigga will."

Jahliya smiled. "Don't let this pussy between my thighs fool you. I got some shit up my sleeve that a man wouldn't even think of. For each hit I want it done a specific way. And you start in two days. But first thing's first. My brother birthday bash is gone be held right here tomorrow night. A few of the guests will be your future targets. You handle this first level and you'll progress to the next. That's when you're start to see your money." She stood up, and sat the dog on the floor. "Get yo man in order. Y'all got two days to be prepared."

***

Stevo paced in the big bedroom with his head down. He was furious, and still dwelling on the fact that Jahliya treated him like a pussy. He felt lower than scum. He punched his fist into his hand.

Makaroni came into the bedroom and stood in the doorway. He checked the hallway to make sure that nobody was around, then he came into the room and closed the door. "Dawg, what's the matter with you?"

"That bitch just treated me like a sucker. I feel like shooting her in the face until my clip is empty."

Makaroni frowned. "Nigga, don't be saying that dumb ass shit about my cousin. You was out of line on this one."

Stevo shot him an angry look. "Aw, so you just meet this bitch and already you're taking her side. What type of shit is that?"

"Nigga, I took yo side the whole way. I told her that she could hold me accountable for what you did. She held me to that, and let that shit go. She really for us to enter into her program so we can start getting this money."

"What program? I ain't finna kiss that bitch ass no matter how much money she got. I'm a man. Men don't bow down to females, Makaroni. You already know we don't."

"Dawg, you sound stupid as hell. Dis shit ain't about bowing down. It's about coming up on some serious paper. I'm tired of being a bum, and I know that you are too. My cousin trying to give us a way out. We gotta take it. All you gotta do

101

is pull that stupid ass attitude in. I ain't trying to be fucked up because of you forever."

That shot cut Stevo deep. "So, tell me how you really feel then. You feel like we been fucked up this long because of me?" He said as low has a whisper.

"Nigga, you be acting like an idiot at times. I gotta admit that. But so do I. That's neither here nor there though. We need to fuck wit' Jahliya so we can get our money right."

Stevo wad still feeling off of what Makaroni said about them being fucked up because of him. He wondered if Makaroni really felt that way deep down. He made some terrible decisions as of late. The robbery with Pam being the biggest. But then there was the hit with Keaira. He shook his head in frustration. "Look, what type of level shit is old girl talking about? Even though I still can't believe that we are about to take orders from a broad."

Makaroni dismissed his last part of the statement. "Look, she want us to prove that we got that killa shit inside of us. So, I guess she finna give us a list of knock offs down here in Memphis. Once we knock them niggas off, we will progress to the next level. She said the next level is where we'll be able to make that paper."

Stevo picked at his chin hairs. He nodded, imagining what needed to be done. Killing had never been a problem for him. "Look, you know I'm down with you, homie. If this is what we finna do, then let's handle our business. I promise that I will refrain from fuckin' it off for us. Aiight?"

Makaroni nodded. "Sound like a plan to me. I just hope you stick to that plan." Makaroni hugged him tight, and let him go.

There was a knock on the door. Montana stuck her head in the room. "Makaroni, can I talk to you for a minute?" She asked looking into his eyes.

He nodded. "Yeah, just give me second."

"Okay." She eased back out of the room.

Stevo exhaled and sat on the bed. "Gone holler at yo sister. I gotta call Keaira. This bitch saying she feeling suicidal. If it ain't one thing it's another."

Makaroni pat him on the back. "I'll see you in a minute."

"N'all, I need to rest. I'll holler at yo ass tomorrow morning. Peace."

***

Makaroni knocked on Montana's bedroom door. She opened it, and smiled when she saw that it was him. She grabbed his wrist and pulled him inside, closing the door behind him.

"Sis, what's good with you?" He asked. He saw that she was dressed in a see-through pink bra, with the matching boy shorts that were designed by Victoria's Secrets.

"Okay. So, I need to get your advice on something." She walked by her big bed and patted it.

Makaroni took a seat. He watched Montana walk to her vanity mirror with her ass cheeks jiggling out of her panties. She stopped in front of it, and popped back on her legs. "What you need my advice on?" He was trying his best to not look down. Sometimes he hated how thick she was. It was hard to not notice.

"So, you already know that Jahliya run one of the biggest strip clubs down here in Memphis called Boss Kittens. Well, she was saying that with the way I'm built that I could work there as a bartender and make some serious money. I mean, she gave me the option of dancing too, but I don't know if I'm good enough for that yet." She turned around to face him. Her panties were all up in her gap.

"So, what are you asking me, Montana?"

She sucked on her bottom lip. Her areolas could be seen clear as day. "I'm asking you if you think that I should do it?"

"Do what?"

She sighed. "Either or?"

"Well, which one do you wanna do?"

She turned around and looked back in the mirror. She arched her back, and popped her ass out. It jiggled. The leg holes traveled further up. She spaced her feet. From this position Makaroni could see her pussy lips. She knew this, and she was hoping he was looking. All of the teasing by Stevo had did something to her. "I don't know. I think the strippers make more money. You seen me dance before. Do you think I could dance?" She walked up on him, and stood before him. She stepped closer until she was in between his legs.

He could smell her perfume coming off of her. "I mean, yeah, you straight. I ain't seen you dance in a long time though. So, I really can't say."

She looked into his eyes. "So, what are you saying? You saying you want me to dance for you right now? I mean, because I would."

Makaroni looked her up and down. He didn't know if it was the weed, or maybe the fact that she was standing so close and smelling so good. But he felt himself getting hard. He didn't feel comfortable with her standing so close while he was in that state.

"Well, what do you want me to do?" She asked enticingly. She rested her hand on his shoulder.

Makaroni was lost. He knew what he should say, but his brain wouldn't allow for him to say it. So, he sat there. Stuck, and speechless.

"You know what? I'm finna just show you a few moves." Montana announced stepping from between his thighs, and going to lock the door. Her panties were deep in her ass crack.

Makaroni noted that as her skin got closer to her ass cheeks it got a tad bit darker. He couldn't believe that he was peeping her like that. He looked on as she locked the door. Then she turned around with a wicked grin on her face. He cleared his throat.

She began walking toward him. "Let me ask you a question, and I want you to be honest. Have you been dreaming about me?"

Ghost

Chapter 12

Makaroni wanted to stick his hands between his thighs so he could adjust himself, but he couldn't. Had he done that, it would have exposed the fact that he was actually aroused. "What do you mean have I been dreaming about you?"

Montana walked up on him, and turned her back so he could see her ass. She waved it from right to left. Then she bent all the way over so he could see her gap underneath. Her ass was inches away from his face. She sat down in his lap. "I want you to be honest with me. If you keep it real with me, I'll tell you what I really been thinking about you." She moved from side to side until she felt his hard dick slip into her crease, and then laid back against him. "Mmm. So, have you?"

Makaroni was embarrassed. He knew that she could feel his pole poking at her. He held her by the side of the ass to steady her. He wanted to build up the nerve to push her off of his lap but the male whore in him wouldn't allow it. It felt too good. His lower self was causing his brain to block out the fact of their relation. "Yeah, you done been in a bunch of my dreams. Why wouldn't you have?" He hissed.

Montana felt the warm air against her earlobe and it made her pussy wet. She opened her thighs wide, and slipped her hand in between them. Her cat felt hot. She imagined Makaroni fucking her from the back. Her nipples spiked against the thin material of her bra. "I done dreamed about you too, big bruh. I think somethin' wrong wit' me because I know damn well I ain't supposed to be looking at you like that. But I can't help it. I think I want you to fuck me." She spun around until she was facing him. She placed one thigh on each side of his own. Looked him in the eyes as if she were seeing him for the first time. Her lips hovered inches from his. "Do you want to?"

Makaroni popped his head back. "Man, stop playin' wit' me. You my mafuckin' sistah." He tried to remove her from his lap gently.

She held on to his shoulders. "I know who I am. But we ain't nowhere near Milwaukee. I say whatever we do down here in Memphis stay down here. If you don't say shit, I won't either. Ain't nobody ever gotta find out." She leaned forward, and kissed his lips softly. Her tongue traced them. Then she sucked on his bottom one.

Makaroni felt like he was harder than he had ever been before. He couldn't believe that Montana wanted to fuck him. He thought that something must've seriously been going wrong inside of her brain. "Shorty, you tripping."

"Am I though?" She slipped her hand between their bodies, and squeezed his hard dick that was peeking out of the waistband of his trousers. "Mack, you are hard as hell right now. You know that you are thinking about sliding this into my tight lil' box. You wanna do this shit as bad as I want you to. Matter fact." She slipped from his lap, and knelt between his legs. She unbuttoned his pants, and pulled them down far enough for his dick to spring straight upward. She grabbed it into her little hand, and began to pump it slowly while her tongue ran across her lips, moistening them.

Makaroni could've easily pushed her away. He was stronger. He knew what they were about to do was wrong. But the excitement in his gut made it feel so right. They were a long way from Milwaukee. He started to buy into the same reasoning that Montana was spitting. What happened outside of Milwaukee stayed outside of Milwaukee.

She sucked him into her mouth, and moaned around the head. She held him with one hand, while her other slipped into her panties. Her sex lips were wet with her dew. She could feel her cream all over her fingers. The hardness of Makaroni's dick in her mouth felt like the greatest feeling in the world. She knew it was wrong. She knew that if anybody found out that they would judge them, and try to shame them to death. But she didn't care. It was taboo. It was saying screw everybody else's opinion. Her truth was that the act drove her crazy. This was her way of fulfilling her fantasy of Makaroni. She felt like fuck the world. She was loving her truth. The world could kiss her ass, and shame the devil.

Makaroni pumped into her mouth from the bed. He had crossed the line. There was no going back. Now he was forced to be all in. He scooted all the way back on the big bed. His big dick popped out of her mouth and stood straight up, dripping her saliva. "Come eat this, lil' sis. You really want me to hit that pussy? Well come get it then."

Montana stood at the foot of the bed, and unhooked her bra from the front. She slid it down her shoulders and dropped it to the floor. "Bruh, you ain't saying nothing but a word. I been wanting to do this." She climbed across the bed with her ass jiggling. She took a hold of his piece again. Licked up it, and sucked all over the head. Then she was sucking him up and down. As far down as she could take him.

Makaroni saw that fat ass in the air, and he couldn't help himself from grabbing some of that booty meat. He slipped his fingers down to her hot crack, and pulled the material to the side, exposing her pussy. The folds were wide, and meaty. His dick jumped in her mouth. He moaned. "You really finna let me fuck you, sis? Huh?"

Montana popped him out. His dick was covered with spit. She stroked him with medium speed. "I need to see what you feel like. I wish we would have done it when we were little and we used to play all of those games. You had me so sticky back then, but I was scared. I can't let this moment pass now."

She sucked him back into her mouth, spearing her face into his crotch at full speed, slurping loudly.

Makaroni was groaning like he was in pain. He still couldn't believe that Montana was doing what she was doing. He started remembering all of the times he'd caught her playing with her kitten when they were little, and she would play it off and act as if she weren't. Then all of the times they would wrestle back then. She would always find a way to get him between her thighs. Once there, she would lock her thighs around his waist and not let him go for the rest of their match. The nipples on her small chest would be as hard as pebbles.

Montana nipped with her teeth. Then she sucked him as hard as she could. His dick jumped. She felt his balls go into his stomach, before the cum came shooting into her orifice.

Makaroni whimpered. His whimpering turned into a groan. He grabbed a handful of her hair, and guided her while she sucked him faster and faster. He couldn't help jerking like crazy.

Montana sat back on her haunches. Her pussy was on display. The material of her panties were bunched to the left side of her box, forcing her sex lips into one another. "How do you feel?" She asked, rubbing between her legs.

Makaroni got on to his knees, and picked her up. He laid her back on the bed, and pushed her knees to her shoulders. "Let me eat this pussy and show you how big bro get down." He lowered his face, and kissed all over her bald lips. His tongue separated the folds. He licked up and down her groove. Her taste was salty, yet sweet to him. He released her knees and slid two fingers into her box, fucking them in and out in fast motion while he sucked on her clit.

"Aw-uh. Aw-uh. Aw-uh. Shit. You gon' make me cum. You gon' make me cum!" She hollered. She opened her thighs wider for him.

Makaroni's fingers were a blur. They made sticky sounds as they flew in and out of her. His tongue made tight circles around her clit again and again. He wanted her to cum. He needed her to cum. He kissed her pearl, and slurped it.

Montana bucked. She covered her face with her hand and screamed as loud as she could. Then she took his head, and forced him to eat her some more. Her thick thighs wrapped around his head while he did his thing. She came back to back. Then she pushed him away, and scooted backward.

Makaroni stood up with his long piece throbbing past his navel. He stroked it. He watched Montana slide her panties off. She opened her thick thighs for him to see her gap. This made him even harder. "I'm finna fuck this pussy hard." He climbed across the bed.

Montana laid on her back, and opened her thighs wider. "Please fuck me hard, big bruh. Treat this pussy. I need that savage shit like I know you be doing them other females."

Makaroni didn't need any more encouragement. He lined himself up, and sank into her womb like a butter knife into warm butter. Her walls locked around him and tried to prevent him from entering her as if it knew the act was wrong. He slammed home, and without missing a beat began to fuck her like a porn star.

Montana dug her nails into his back. She wrapped her ankles around his waist, and fell in love with the way he was pounding her out. The headboard tapped against the wall as he dug her out. She sucked on his neck, moaning in his ear. "Aw-uh. Aw-uh. Ooo shit. Wait, bruh. You too... Ooo... Deep. You so deep. Awww, my big broth... Is... Fucking... Meeee-yah!" She moaned, and came.

Makaroni flipped her over, and pulled her up by her hips. He pushed her face to the mattress, and got to fucking her with all of his might again. He watched his piece go in and out of her. "Dis mine. Dis my pussy. Huh. Huh. Huh. You hear me?" He growled.

Montana had her face laying on the sheets, getting her pussy beat in. It felt so good that she couldn't speak. All she could do was yelp every time he hit a deep spot in her that had never been hit before. His hard pipe felt like a million-dollar lottery ticket to her.

"You steady talking. Dat. Uh. Uh. Stripper shit." He smacked her ass hard. "Fuck me like one. Twerk, sis." He rammed into her harder and harder.

Montana's face moved up and down the sheet. She spread her knees, and began to pop in his lap. Their skins met to create a loud collision each time. It sounded like a round of applause was being given. The stronger she pushed back on Makaroni, the deeper he went inside of her. She came when he smacked her ass again.

Makaroni felt himself about to cum. He pulled out, and flipped Montana over. Opened her thighs, and came all over her fat pussy and stomach. "Uh. Uh. Uhhhh." He groaned as it shot out of him. Then he was running his head all over her sex lips.

Montana laid there with her legs spread. She was breathing heavily. Sweat peppered her chest. She could feel his hot semen all over her. It drove her crazy. Then he fell beside her breathing just as hard. Montana grabbed him and kissed his lips. "I love you, Makaroni. I love you so fucking much that it ain't funny."

Makaroni didn't know what to say or do. He kissed her back, and closed his eyes. "We lucky it's a shower in this mafucka or else we'd be popped."

Montana laughed. "We gotta open up a window before our scent leak into the hallway."

Now Makaroni was laughing. "Hell yeah, we do."

***

After their shower, Montana crawled in the bed naked. She climbed on top of Makaroni with her freshly washed pussy on top of his dick. She humped into it for a few moments until it was hard, then slid it into her box. Her eyes rolled into the back of her head. She was sore, but she couldn't get enough of him. She laid on his chest. "Are you okay, Makaroni?"

Makaroni gripped her ass. "I'm good. I'm thankful that Jahliya been out of the mansion all night, and that Stevo was knocked out when I went downstairs to check on him. I don't think we could've explained what we just did. We made a lot of noise."

Montana giggled. "I know we did. That's your fault though. I didn't think you was gon' fuck me like that."

"That's what you asked me to do." He gripped her booty. "You got any regrets?"

She shook her head. "Nope. Only I wish we were at a hotel or something so we could go at it again. It'll be kind of dangerous to do that right now." She rode him real slow for a few moments, the stopped, laying her hard nipples against his chest. "I hope we can do this all the time, Makaroni. You know, as long as we ain't in Milwaukee, of course." She snickered.

Makaroni held her for a second. "I don't know about that. I guess we will see. For now, let's just enjoy what we did. Tomorrow is a new day. I gotta get up." He smacked her on the booty, and rolled her off of him. His piece slipped out of her hole with a low popping sound. He stood on the side of the bed. "I'll see you in the morning, okay?"

She nodded. "Yeah, okay."

"Aiight." He walked to the door and grabbed the handle.

"Wait." Montana hopped out of the bed and ran up to him. She grabbed his face, and tongued him down. Then stepped back with her secretions running down her thighs. "Okay, now you can go."

Makaroni didn't know what to make of what she had just done so he didn't say anything at all. What had taken place had taken place. That was that. *Tomorrow presented a new day*, he thought.

Chapter 13

Stevo stepped in front of the full-length mirror. He was dressed in a black and white Supreme outfit with matching Balenciaga shoes that Jahliya had bought for him. His dreads were freshly twisted. He had gotten a nice lining from a traveling barber that she had come to the mansion, and he was fresh out of the shower. He felt like a Boss. All he was missing was a little water for his neck and wrist so he could be dripping.

Makaroni stepped into the room with his waves popping. They were freshly cut, and edged. He was wearing a black and blue Yves Saint Laurent fit with matching Balenciaga's. He slipped a pair of Chanel glasses on his face, cross-dressing designers, and stood beside Stevo, handing him a pair of Ray Bans. "Huh, nigga, you gon' need these if you tryna stand next to a boss ass nigga like me." He joked.

Stevo smacked his lips. "Nigga, please. You still just as broke as me. You ain't got no coin in yo pocket." He slowly placed the non-prescription glasses over his eyes, and looked into the mirror. "Yeah, now we talking. I look like a finer version of Quavo."

Makaroni waved him off. "Nigga, I look like a version of me. Fuck Quavo."

Jahliya stepped into the room from the hallway. "Slow y'all roll, players. Both of you look handsome. Now it's time to play the part. These designer clothes ain't gon' be nothing if y'all past this next stage. This shit gon' be light work. Trust me when I tell you that." She walked up to Makaroni and kissed him on the cheek. "You smell good too." She smiled.

"Shid, what about me? I know I ain't family and all that, but you gotta give a nigga props when he looking and smelling dis mafuckin' good."

She smiled. "Dat's the thing though. Playboy, this is the south. Down here we tend to complement our own, and enjoy our own before we step outside of us. But you smell good though." She turned to Makaroni and dusted a piece of lint off of his suit. "JaMichael a be here in a few hours. He can't wait to meet you. You are all he's been talking about." She pulled a swollen stuffed blunt from her shirt pocket, and sparked it. A thick line of smoke drifted to the ceiling. "Y'all remember now that it's going to be a few players here tonight that you are going to have to take care of within the next week or so. So, hug the darkness, and stay vigilant. That's an order. I will let you know who a few of the targets will be. Later, boys." She walked out of the room with her ass jiggling inside of her Gucci skirt.

Stevo couldn't take his eyes off of that ass. He wondered how she got down in the sack. He could tell she was a pure animal in every sense of the word. "Dawg, yo cousin fine as a muthafucka. You ain't notice the way her ass was jiggling in that skirt?"

Makaroni gave him a dumb look. "Nigga, that's my cousin. What the fuck do I look like?"

Stevo smacked his forehead. "Damn, I'm bugging. I wasn't thinking clearly. That's my fault. But she is fine though. Can you at least admit that?"

Makaroni shook his head. "Nigga, n'all. That's my cousin. I can't even look at her like that." He lied. In actuality it was impossible for him to not notice how righteous Jahliya was fitting that skirt. She was too thick. Every time she walked her ass jiggled. He was trying to not think about it though, and he most definitely didn't want Stevo to know his thoughts. He knew his right-hand man would have a whole lot to say.

"Yeah, well, I'm glad she ain't mine 'cause I'm most definitely finna try my luck. The worst thing she can say is no.

But the best thing she can do is let me fuck at least once." He laughed imagining bending Jahliya over and fucking her from the back.

Makaroni stepped beside him. "Look, nigga. You said that you wasn't going to fuck this up for us. If you come at my cousin, that's exactly what you're going to do, so I'ma have to ask you to back off until we get our money right. You got a problem wit' that?"

Stevo turned to face him. "Dawg, what? You cuffing family members now?"

"Hell n'all. Fuck I look like? This is about business. That's it."

Stevo stared into Makaroni's eyes for a long time. Then he sucked his teeth. "Fuck that bitch then. It's plenty Southern pussy down here. I'll just smash one of those Eaters." He turned away from Makaroni, and stepped back into the mirror. "Besides, I gave you my word that I wasn't going to fuck anything up, so I won't."

Makaroni came and rested his hand on his shoulder. "Look, homie. I just wanna see us with some serious paper. That's it. We both tired of being broke. In order for us to get over the hump, we gotta handle our business the right way. You can get on that dumb shit later."

Stevo curled his upper lip, and looked at Makaroni through the mirror. "And I most definitely will. You betta believe that."

***

JaMichael pulled up in a cherry red Range Rover two hours later. He jumped out of the truck, and dusted off his Chanel fit. Stomped his boots on the ground to get weed ashes off of him. There was a purple stain on his right pant leg from where the Syrup had dropped on him. He picked at it, and shrugged once he saw that he couldn't get it out. He had two bodyguards step out behind him. They were armed with Tech .9s.

Jahliya opened the big mansion doors and took off running to him. She jumped into his arms. He held her. Kissed her forehead, and sat her back on the ground. "Damn, boy. What took you so long to get here?" She asked suddenly irritated.

JaMichael was gone off of two Percocet sixties, and a quarter bottle of Lean. He wiped his mouth, and struggled to keep his eyes open. "Shawty, you already know how Nikki get whenever she get a mafucka down there in Houston wit' her ass. She acted like she didn't wanna let me go." He shook his head. "Den Bubbie got to tripping about the twins."

Jahliya frowned. "Yeah, nigga, I don't care about none of dat shit. You here now so let's just chill."

Makaroni stood in front of the mansion beside Stevo, watching the entire scene unfold. He was trying to see if he recognized JaMichael but he didn't. He also noticed the way Jahliya seemed to soften at the sight of her little brother. He thought that was cool.

JaMichael walked up to him with his hand out. "What's good, lil' cuz?" He shook his hand and gave him a half-hug.

Makaroni accepted it. He could smell the drank and weed all over JaMichael. "Long time no see I guess."

"Yeah. Right." JaMichael laughed. He mugged Stevo. "Who is dis nigga?"

"Aw, shit. Dis my nigga—" Makaroni started.

"Stevo, homie. Dat's who I am. Dis my brother right here. We locked in like cell mates. You feel me."

JaMichael nodded. "Dat's what's up. Let's go inside so we can get this show on the road."

***

An hour later, JaMichael loaded Makaroni and Stevo into his Escalade and pulled down the long driveway with a Draco on his lap. He had a car follow them that had two ex-police officers on security. "Look, Mane, dis shit gon' be real simple here, Playboys. Y'all gon' knock a few of these Memphis nig-gas' heads off, and head back up north with a nice bag, and a plug on the Rebirth. You know what the Rebirth is?" He asked them.

Makaroni had heard Mike's rumblings about a product called the Rebirth. It was supposed to be a form of heroin that was chemically enhanced, and cut with Fentanyl. It was cre-ated to get the addicts as high as they had ever been. Also, to make the addicts so addicted to the product that they would give up anything to have it. Makaroni had always heard the stories about their older cousin Taurus and how he got rich off of that product while messing around with some Russian fe-male. "Yeah, I heard a lil' bit about that. Yo Pops brought that shit to the hood, right?"

"Taurus the Great, you muthafuckin' right he did. He paved the way for me and my sister to take over the Game, and that's what we are doing, and going to continue to do. Ain't no other way around it."

"Well, I don't have the slightest clue of what The Rebirth is so please somebody enlighten me." Stevo chimed in.

"You wanna answer that for him, Makaroni?" JaMichael asked.

Makaroni cleared his throat. "Well, I honestly only got a small understanding of what it is, but as far as I know, it's a highly addictive form of that Boy. It's so addictive that it be having them feens ready to do whatever for it. My cousin Tau-rus, which is JaMichael's father, is the one that brought it down to Memphis back in the day. That's how he got rich and was able to leave that generational money behind for both Jahliya and JaMichael."

JaMichael smiled. "My pops was a mafuckin' man. I miss him."

"Why you talking about him in the past tense? Where is he now?" Stevo asked.

JaMichael kept rolling. He felt a sudden sense of sickness. "My old man was put to death back in twebty-eighteen."

"Damn. I'm sorry to hear that." Stevo said giving him his condolences.

"The family dealing with it. It's still a process." JaMichael grabbed his bottle of Pink Sprite. It was Codeine and Promethazine. He sipped from it. He exhaled to release the pain from his soul. "Anyway, let's get off all of that sappy shit for a minute. We got a problem. More like an infestation down here in Memphis that I gotta have you two lil' niggas take care of like ASAP. That is going to be your first level to pass so you can get into to good graces with both myself and Jahliya."

Stevo perked up in the backseat. "What you talking about? I mean we can say fuck yo party tonight and go and handle this business right now."

"Yeah, bruh, I really don't feel like partying no way. I want me and the homie to get this show on the road. The sooner we exterminate these mafuckas that you talking about, the sooner we can get on to the next level where we will be able to get our money right." Makaroni backed Stevo up.

JaMichael pulled up to a stop light, and looked to them. "Aw, so y'all saying that y'all don't wanna celebrate my late birthday, and coming home from the Feds party wit' me?"

"On some real shit?" Makaroni asked.

"Yeah." JaMichael wanted to know.

"Hell n'all." Stevo took over.

"Nigga, we ain't got shit to celebrate. We broke. We ain't got a pot to piss in. We are all the way down here from Milwaukee trying to get put on. Mafuckas on a mission. Once we get right then we can celebrate, but not until then." Makaroni said.

JaMichael nodded. "Okay den, lil' niggas. Well that's good because shit starts right now. I'm finna roll y'all somewhere. When we get there, y'all finna jump out on business wit' no questions asked. It's a few lil' niggas that act like they don't think fat meat is greasy. We gon' show 'em different. Check under those seats. Both of y'all should have a Mach .90 under them mafuckas."

Makaroni grabbed his from under his seat. It was all chrome. It felt heavy in his hands. He took the clip out, and slammed it back in. "How many shots I'm working wit'?"

"Eighty." JaMichael answered. "Dem bitches brand-new too. Well oiled, and ready to go. Military issued. Only the best for my Hittas. That's why I got y'all rolling wit' eighty shots."

"Depending on how many niggas we bucking at, I might not need that many." Stevo jacked. "Where the masks at?"

"Under the seat as well." JaMichael got off of the highway and wound up in a seedy section of the Orange Mound. He smiled. "Dis my old stomping grounds right here. Now I just look to conquer this mafucka. Now it's very important that when y'all jump out and handle yo business that you scream White Haven more than once. You got me?"

"Who the fuck is White Haven?" Stevo asked.

"You let me worry about that. Just do like I say." JaMichael said looking back at him. He turned on to a street that turned into a winding road. On each side of the road were red bricked row houses. Though it was only forty degrees outside, there were a lot of people out. "Aiight, now we finna roll past a group of young niggas that's out here hussling. They gon' be on our left, right up here. Count how many it is, and devise your plan of attack right away. I'ma drop y'all off at the corner store up that way so y'all can go back and handle yo business.

When you air them niggas out, hit it through the first gangway you see, and take the alley leading back up to the corner store. It's only one. I'ma meet you right in that alley. That'll be mission complete."

Stevo was ready to go. "Sound like a plan to me."

JaMichael nodded at the group of Dope Boys as his Range Rover with the major tints rolled past. He clenched his jaw out of anger. These were young savages that refused to fall under his Régime's rule. Savages that he needed to get rid of along with a few choice others. "Y'all see them bitch ass niggas?" He asked.

Both Stevo and Makaroni nodded. They each clutched their Machs, ready. There was a silence in the car that brought both a calm and excitement. Both men wanted to get the job done and over with.

JaMichael rolled to the corner store, and into the alley beside it. He rolled down it a bit, and stopped. "I'ma be right here. Y'all gon' and handle that business. Remember to keep screaming White Haven. Hurry up."

"Let's get it, Stevo!" Makaroni hollered jumping out of the truck.

Stevo cocked his Mach, and jumped out beside Makaroni. He situated his mask, ready for action.

Chapter 14

Makaroni ducked on the side of the row house. About fifty feet away from him stood a crowd of Dope Boys. They were drinking bottles of Promethazine. Smoking Newport cigarettes, and popping their bags of Boy. Makaroni counted nine of them. Each one had on a puffy coat. Directly across the parking lot from where he was kneeling, he could hear the sounds of the new Moneybagg album banging from one of the windows that he couldn't quite pinpoint. His finger wavered on the Mach, itching to get to fucking it like he'd done Montana's pussy.

Stevo breathed out a gasp of air as he crouched down beside him. He got as close to the brick wall as he could. He eyed the group of Dope Boys with hatred. Even though he didn't know them he hated them because they were standing in his way of moving forward in the Game. "Nigga, you ready?"

Makaroni lowered his eyes. He looked from right to left to scan the neighborhood one more time. Then he nodded. "Let's get it."

Stevo jumped up, and ran forty of the fifty feet, and stopped. He extended his Mach .90. "White Haven, fuck niggas!" *Boom. Boom. Boom. Boom.*

Makaroni stepped beside him pulling his trigger as well. The bullets zipped from the gun and with precision sliced into four different Dope Boys right away. He watched the skin enter their necks, and exit through their jaws. They fell, and he kept spitting.

Stevo chased behind two of the Dope Boys that he hit up in the back. They staggered but continued to run on wobbly legs. One crashed into a car that was parked in the middle of the street. Stevo was on him. He slammed the Mach into the back of his head and held the trigger. The Dope Boy's head exploded all over his mask. He slumped to his knees before fell face-first into the ground.

The second one staggered and tripped over the curb. The bullets had pierced his lungs. He struggled to breathe. He fell onto his side scratching at the brown grass, wondering what was happening to him.

Stevo stood over him with no remorse. "White Haven, nigga." He pumped four into his face, and turned around to see what Makaroni was doing.

Makaroni ran eighty paces down the street, chasing behind a heavy-set Dope Boy that had dropped his pistol. He bucked and knocked a hefty chunk out of his thigh. Then bucked again and caught him in the back. He fell, paralyzed. Makaroni rushed up to him and stood over him. "Dis White Haven, nigga. Remember that." He raised his foot to stomp him twice in the face. Neglecting to kill him. Then he was taking off behind Stevo, and down the alley. They left Orange Mound was in a frenzy.

***

Makaroni laid on his back, staring at the ceiling of his bedroom inside of Jahliya's mansion. He could hear the party for JaMichael going on downstairs and he didn't want any parts of it. His mind was spinning out of control. He kept replaying the images of death from earlier that day. He exhaled and shook his head. He wondered what the Game was really all about, and if most of the Kingpins, or rich Bosses in it had to endure as much as he and Stevo had to before they got major.

Montana stuck her head inside of the room. "Mack, what's good, Playboy? Why you ain't downstairs enjoying JaMichael bash? It's all kinds of bad ass strippers down there."

"I'm good, Shorty. Y'all have fun." He closed his eyes, and drifted off into the recesses of his own mind. More images of the Mach blasts replayed themselves before his eyelids. He saw the blood. He saw the brain matter. He even could remember the sounds of the screaming coming from the Dope Boys as the bullets ate into their flesh, and knocked huge chunks of meat from them.

Montana locked the door. She came and laid on the bed next to him. She turned to look at her brother, and felt a sudden case of worry. "I'd pay a penny for your thoughts, Mack."

Makaroni opened his eyes. "Why shit gotta be so hard, Montana?"

That question caught her off guard. "What do you mean?"

"Life, Shorty." He sat up. "Fuck." Then he stood. "It seemed like we been dealt a shitty hand since birth. Ever since Pops punk ass cut out on us for his punk ass family in Wauwatosa."

Montana sat up. "Makaroni, what happened tonight?"

He started to pace. "Nothin'. We just got into some bullshit. Business needed to be taken care of, and that's what it was." He paced, lost in his mind again.

Montana stood up. "Bruh, can you talk to me like I'm your sister? I mean I get that we did what we did, but I'm still your lil' sister. We are still in this shit together, no matter where we are. Now I know you need to talk, so let's do it."

Makaroni had a heavy heart. He was tired of being a bottom feeder. He was growing addicted to killing, and his remorse was leaving him. He didn't know how to tell Montana that. She was still just a female, even if she was his kid sister. "Look, it's hard to explain the Game to you. But your brother got plans to move up through the ranks. I ain't gon' be this bum ass nigga that you see right now. I'm taking the steps to become what I need to become for our people. Tonight just got me to thinking a lil' bit."

"Does it have anything to do with what's been all over Facebook?" She asked softly.

"What do you mean?" He felt nervous.

"Well, today, there was a mass shooting over there on the Orange Mound. Like eight people got killed. Another was left for dead and he is in the hospital with serious injuries. They don't know if he's going to make it either. So, is that it?"

Makaroni had never lied to Montana before in his life. He didn't want it to be the first time. "Sis, the less you know about everything the better." He turned his back to her.

She stepped around, and into his face. "Fuck that, Makaroni. I just told you that we are in this shit together. You ain't alone, and the way I see it, you did what you had to do. If it was up to me and I was a man, I would do the same things to make sure that I was becoming a King instead of a straight fuckin' loser. Fuck them niggas that died today. It is what it is. We ain't never been soft, and all we know how to go is hard. That will never change. You hear me?"

Makaroni hung his head. He didn't know how to respond. He was still feeling a bit sick. He wondered if it was because of how many spirits he had on his soul after taking so many lives.

Montana grabbed him by the chin. "Nigga, I said did you hear me?" She growled.

Makaroni snatched her up, and threw her on the bed. He got between her thighs, and yanked her Prada dress up roughly. Then he ripped her panties off, and threw them over his shoulders. In seconds he slid nine inches deep into her wet pussy and was fucking her hard enough to get rid of his frustrations. "You wanna fuck wit' a killa? Huh, sis? Dis what you want?"

Montana was licking all over his face. She sucked his neck, then bit into it hard enough to draw blood. This made Makaroni fuck her faster and deeper. She moaned, and kept right on licking all over him. "I love you. I swear to God I do, Mack."

"Huh. Huh. Huh. You too. Montana. Sis. You too." He sped up the pace. Sucked all over her cheeks, and neck. He popped her titties out. Then his tongue made circles around each areola. He sucked them hungrily.

Montana wrapped her arms around his neck, and screamed. She came pulling him down to her. Makaroni was piping her so fast that she couldn't think straight. Before she knew it, she was cuming again, bucking up into him.

Makaroni slowed his pace, and started to make love to her tight pussy. At this pace he could feel her walls sucking at him. They were tugging over and over. It felt so good that he couldn't help shivering. "When I come up, Montana, I'ma spoil you." More stroking. His dick grew another inch unbeknownst to him. He hit her bottom back to back. "You hear me, lil' baby."

"Unnnn, yes. Yes. I do." She moaned with her thighs splayed wide open. Every time Makaroni would crash into her box it sent a jolt of electricity all the way from her clitoris to her brain. He had her fallen into an abyss of uncertainty. "I love you."

He sucked all over her breasts. Smushed them together. He took time to cherish each nipple one at a time. His hips continued to drive his piece in and out of her box. "You ain't never supposed to want for shit. You shouldn't have to wear some shit that Jahliya bought you. That's what you got me for." He kept his pace slow and steady.

Montana laid back and allowed for him to do whatever he wanted to do to her. It felt so good. She felt so special. She didn't care how wrong the act was. A voice kept repeating in her mind to fuck the world. That's how she felt. "I know you gon' take care of me, Makaroni. I know you is. I'ma come up, too. I'ma be a boss, too."

Makaroni liked hearing that. He knew that they were destined for greatness. They had been through too much hardship to not come out on top. He flipped her onto her stomach and laid on top of her ass cheeks. She spaced her thick thighs. He sunk back into her hot pussy and kept fucking. His speed increased just a tad.

Montana sucked on her fist. With every forward thrust she felt like she was on the verge of cuming. She couldn't believe that Makaroni was having such an impact on her, but he was. She wished that they could've stayed tangled up in the bed forever.

Makaroni bit into the back of her neck. He sent chills down her spine. "You gon' be my baby? Huh?"

She nodded. "Yeah. Even when we get back to Milwaukee. You can have this anytime you want it. I'm yours. I promise."

Makaroni laid her on her side, and snuggled up to her ass. He slid back into her and kept fucking. "I killed a bunch of niggas today, sis. I laid they bitch ass down. I had to. I gotta make it to the next phase. I just got to. For us."

"I get it. I swear I get it." She moaned and sucked on her bottom lip as a tremor went through her pussy and left her shaking.

"I just needed to tell somebody. I got too much pressure—" His eyes rolled backward. He felt himself about to cum. He sped up as fast as he could. Before it shot out of him, he pulled out, rolled Montana on her stomach and came all over her ass cheeks. It felt like warm candle wax. Drip after drip.

"Mmm! That feel so good." She humped into the bed sheets. Her fingers snuck into her box. She diddled her clit until she came again, whimpering his name.

Makaroni rubbed all over her ass. His nut disappeared like lotion. He pulled Montana up and sat on the bed beside her. "Listen to me, sis. I got us. I need to buss a few more moves down in Memphis. When I get back to Milwaukee, we finna ball hard. I promise you that. Just stay under Jahliya and pick her brain. I'ma do the same to JaMichael. Aiight?"

In response she grabbed him to her, and kissed his lips. She sucked them as if it were going to be their last kiss. When they separated, she felt emotional. She tried desperately to not show Makaroni that though. She didn't want to make things even more complicated. "All you need to know, Mack, is that I'm riding wit' you, ten toes down. I got you."

***

Stevo took one last swallow of his Hennessey, and dropped the empty paper cup into the trashcan. He made his way through the raging party until he eased upon Jahliya. She was coming from the hallway with a peculiar smile on her face. He stepped in front of her. "How you doing, Goddess?"

She smacked her lips. "Boy, busy. Excuse me." She tried to step around him.

He blocked her path again. "Wait a minute. I wanted to ask you something."

The music was blaring so loud that he could barely hear himself. There were strippers all over the party with crowds of men around them while they performed. Loads of dollar bills scattered the floors. JaMichael sat at the front of the mansion inside of a Golden Throne. He even had a crown on his head, cheering on three strippers that were in front of him. Two of Jahliya's bodyguards appeared from the crowd and stood beside her.

Stevo looked up at them with a mug on his face. "Fuck y'all want?" He snapped. "Can't y'all see that I'm trying to have a conversation with this Queen right here?" He felt himself becoming heated.

Jahliya laughed. She gave the order to one of her bodyguards to watch them from a distance. She told him that she didn't want to ruin her brother's bash. Both bodyguards eased back into the crowd. She walked closer to Stevo. "Come on, let's step outside on the veranda so we can talk."

Stevo followed close behind her. He couldn't help watching the way her ass jiggled with each step that she took. He felt that Jahliya was one of the finest females he had ever seen in his life. Before he left Memphis, he was going to do everything that he could to get some of that pussy.

They stepped outside, and Jahliya closed the door behind him. She placed a tuft of her curly hair behind her ear, and signaled to her Shooter in the upstairs window to remain vigilant. "Okay, Stevo, now that you have me alone, ask me your question."

Stevo couldn't take his eyes off of her sexy lips. Her beauty was affecting his train of thought. "Look, Shorty, I'm only in town for a few weeks. I'm feeling you. I like yo drip. I'm tryna get wet. What's good?"

Jahliya laughed. "You telling me that's your pitch for me?" She laughed again. "Look, Stevo, I'm out of your league. When I look at you as the Boss bitch that I am, I don't see any ways in which you could elevate me in any fashion. I don't see a step up, but I do see a pull-me-down. A dependent. Because you don't have anything figured out. Until you can step yo financial and ambition game up, you can miss the notion that you could ever have a chance with me. My pussy is priceless. You understand that? Now it's a bunch of low life stripper bitches inside that a love to take you up on that offer that you proposed to me. They gon' want them blue faces though, so, huh." She pulled a knot of hundreds out of her bra, and handed him one. "Dis on me, Boo." She kissed his cheek and left him looking like a damn fool on the veranda. The scent of her perfume left as a reminder that she was there.

Stevo hung his head. "Fuck you then." He balled the hundred-dollar bill into his fist, and threw it as far into the lawn as he could. "I don't need yo charity!" He snapped. He was so tired of feeling and being treated like shit. He stood on the veranda for ten minutes watching the hundred-dollar bill blow around a bit. Then he opened the door to the party, stepped inside. Before he closed the door back, he turned around, and hopped the railing to retrieve the money that Jahliya had given him. With each step he took toward it, he felt lower and lower.

Ghost

Chapter 15

"Yo, dis bitch drive like we floating on air. I can't wait to get my money all the way up so a nigga can roll one of these bitches on a regular." Makaroni said stepping on the gas to the Hellcat, zooming down the speedway at a hundred miles an hour. When he got to the winding of the road he slowed down. As soon as it straightened out, he was back flooring it with his mouth wide open in fascination.

JaMichael sat in the passenger's seat smoking on a stuffed Syracuse Orange blunt. His eyes were low. He was gone off of two Percocet and a Oxy pill. He felt mellow. "Yeah, well, lil' cuz, you and yo homeboys keep following my commands and y'all a be riding one of these bitches in no time. The game come in steps. Ain't no mafucka that's major ever woke up one day and became a King Pin. You feel me?"

Makaroni nodded. "I hear you. But let me ask you a question. Since Taurus was a major nigga in the South, didn't you kids step into yo Boss role? I mean, how much work did you honestly have to put in?"

JaMichael laughed. He took a few tokes of his blunt, and inhaled it deeply. Then he blew the smoke to the ceiling. "Nigga, we don't believe in handouts. Even though my Pops was who he was, I had to work hard for everything that I got. Me and my sister. These niggas know who I am out here in these streets, lil' cuz. Mafuckas done made movies about this Heartless Goon. Look it up."

Makaroni got the impression that JaMichael was feeling offended. He wanted to nip that in the bud right away. "Look, cuz, I didn't mean for you to take that shit the wrong way. I was just wondering. I know when shit do take off for me and my homeboy that I can't see myself not giving my son the key to the streets as soon as he's old enough."

JaMichael looked him over. "Cuz, if you do shit right, then you won't have to worry about your son having to slang shit like we do? I mean, even for me and Jahliya, we are bigger than the dope game now. It's all about other long term, legal aspects of the hustle. The dope game has always been short term. You gotta get your bread up so you can enroll into college. Learn that real estate trade. Me, I'm jumping off into the movies. That's where my heart is at. You know, beside conquering Memphis."

Makaroni slowed the Hellcat. "That's what's up. But before I can do any of that positive shit, I need you and Jahliya to bless me. So, what's next on the agenda?"

JaMichael looked up ahead. They were approximately thirty seconds from pulling up to the office station of the Midway track. "You remember the mafucka that came out here and gave us the go ahead to spin this track a few times?" He asked looking out of the window.

"Yeah, what about him?"

"Last time I came through this bitch I had Jahliya wit' me. This mafucka acted like he couldn't keep his eyes or his comments to himself. I'ma have you take a good look at his ass while I sit back and enjoy the view." He handed him a wire. "We going into his office."

Makaroni jerked his head back. "Bruh, what that got to do wit' me and my mans advancing in the Game? I ain't trying to be whacking mafuckas just on the strength." He slid the wire into his pocket, and slowed the speed to the Hellcat even more.

JaMichael exhaled loudly. "Second to his disrespectful antics, this mafucka holds the deeds to a bunch of property in the Orange Mound area. I'm talking more than he is supposed to have. It's a lot of struggling sistahs out there. Sistahs that have a hard time paying the rent that he keep on raising. His punk ass take pride in making them do some of the most grotesque things that you can think of. He's sick. A predator. So not only will this help you to reach the next level, but this will be a boost for yourself and Stevo. What you thank bout that?"

Makaroni pulled up in front of the heavyset white man. He looked out at him and imagined him forcing his mother into a compromising position just because she couldn't pay the rent. In an instant, his heart grew as cold as ice for him. "Let me get that boost. This shit gon' be light work."

JaMichael laughed. "Boy, I see a whole lot of me in you. You got that by any means necessary attitude. I like that. Come on."

***

Stevo tapped on the bedroom door that Montana was occupying while she stayed with Jahliya. It was less than two minutes prior to him knocking that he'd seen her go inside of the room. He was feeling horny. He imagined fucking her and it made his pipe jump.

Montana opened the door in a pair of Daisy Duke denim shorts, and a white beater that had the word Boss written across the front of it. Stevo could see that she didn't have any bra on. Her hard nipples poked up against the shirt. "What's good, Stevo?"

Stevo licked his lips. "Fuck you mean what's good? I'm saying, a nigga tryna get a quickie right fast before Makaroni get back. What's up?"

Montana sucked her teeth. "Nigga, that's what you beating on my door for? Really?"

"I ain't beat. I gently knocked on yo shit."

She rolled her eyes. "Look, Stevo, that shit ain't happening no more. It was disrespectful for us to go behind Makaroni's back, doing what we did. I ain't been feeling good about it, so that's done with." She looked down at the carpet, then back up to him. "Is there anything else I can help you with?"

Stevo frowned. He felt like calling her a bitch. She was lucky that she was Makaroni's sister. Even though she had a nice shot on her, he didn't want her thinking that she was God's gift to all men. "Shorty, you serious?"

"Bye, Stevo." She slammed the door in his face.

Stevo took a step back, fuming. "Fuck you den."

Jahliya walked past him in a pair of Chanel jeans that were so tight he wondered how she was able to breathe in them. She looked at him and smiled. "Good evening."

He ignored her, and walked away from Montana's door. Stepped into his room, and laid out on the bed seething. He hated Memphis. He couldn't wait to get back to Milwaukee.

***

"So, what you are saying, Geoffrey, is that you are planning on getting rid of sixty percent of the properties that you possess in Orange Mound?" JaMichael asked in disbelief. "What gives?"

Geoffrey took a seat behind his big desk, and lowered his head. "Uh, if I gotta be honest with you, JaMichael, there are a few women that have waged complaints against me. I haven't done anything that they can prove. But still, I'm just figuring that if I can unload that property to somebody else then all of the heat would die down." He scratched the bald spot that was in the middle of his head.

JaMichael shook his head at Makaroni, giving him the signal to hold fast with the plot to kill the man. He wanted to first find a way to get the properties from him before he dumped them on another man that was just like himself. "What else?"

"And to be further honest with you, the state of Tennessee has red zoned the Orange Mound." Geoffrey said.

"Red zone. What do you mean?" JaMichael asked. He wanted to get a broader understanding.

"Well, son, case you didn't know—" He began.

"Don't call me son. My Pops resting in peace." JaMichael snapped.

"Hey, I'm sorry. No offense meant." Geoffrey submitted.

"Continue." JaMichael ordered.

Geoffrey suddenly felt uneasy. "Red zoning is when the state has agreed to allow for an area in a certain city to rot and decay. It holds back its public responses purposely. So, the police will take their time getting there. So will fire engines when there are serious fires, and ambulances. Also, anybody, but specifically minority men that does so happen to enter into the criminal justice system from that area will be prosecuted to the fullest extent of the law. Government assistance will also be hard to come by for the women. It means that the government has a plan in place for the area to sink as low as it can go, before they run everybody out to other parts of Memphis."

JaMichael sat there with a mug on his face. He was furious. He couldn't believe that real things like that actually existed. "So pretty much, you are bailing before it all goes down. Am I correct?"

Geoffrey shrugged. "I guess you can say that."

"And you're serious about all this?" JaMichael pushed further.

He grabbed a bunch of paperwork and deeds out of his desk. "Does this look like I'm joking?" He slid them across the table to JaMichael. "You make me an offer in the millions right now and you can have them son of a bitch properties right now, or as soon as the paperwork goes through. All it a takes is my signature and it's all yours. So, what is your first offer."

JaMichael continued to peruse the paperwork. Sure enough, all it would take was for Geoffrey to sign on the dotted line and all of the property could be JaMichael's. His mouth began to salivate. "I'll give you two million for everything. And I'm talking cash. Them people ain't even gotta be in our business. Or I can give you a million cash, and a million-wire transfer. How do you want it?"

Geoffrey couldn't believe his luck. He felt that JaMichael must've really been an idiot. Hadn't he just told him that they were looking to tear the entire area down? He would have easily accepted a million even, but two was always better than one. "I'll take one and one. That way uncle Sam thinks that a legit sale was made. And the other one I will have fun with. We can finalize this at your earliest convenience."

JaMichael stood up. "We finna do this shit today. I want your name on those dotted lines before the sun goes down. You feel me?"

Geoffrey sat back, and kicked his feet up on the desk with a smile on his face. "Then you go ahead and do what you have to. I'm ready when you are." He said in his strong country accent.

***

Later that night, Makaroni, Montana, Jahliya, and JaMichael wound up at the cemetery standing inside of the mausoleum where Blaze, Princess, and most recently Taurus's body had been buried. It was three years since Blaze and Princess had been murdered, and almost two years since Taurus had been put to death.

Jahliya stepped in front of Princess's stone, and rubbed the lettering. She missed her mother even though she had never really had the appropriate chance to get to know her the right way. She was only a little girl of four when she was killed. "Mama, I swear, even though I was robbed of the chance to really get to know you, I'm going hard for you down here and I will never forget you. I love you. I just wanted to be here on your death anniversary to let you know exactly that." She kissed the stone.

Montana rested her head on her shoulder. She could only imagine what she was going through. When she thought about somebody hurting Maisey, the thought was enough to drive her insane. "I got you, cuz."

JaMichael took a deep breath and tipped a bottle of Rosé as he looked over Blaze's burial space. "I love you, mama. You already know that yo baby boy going hard. You live inside of me. Always have. Always will."

Makaroni felt uneasy inside of the mausoleum. He knew that everybody had to die. He wondered how he was going to go out, and when it would be. He lived a fast life. As much as he hated to admit it, he was afraid of death. Not death itself but the fear of how he was going to go out terrified him. He just prayed that when the Reaper came, he was able to leave behind a whole bunch of money for his sister and mother. That was all that mattered to him.

They huddled up in front of Taurus's space in silence for a long time. It felt cold inside of the mausoleum. It felt creepy. All four couldn't wait to get out of there.

"Pops, we love you, Mane. Yo blood run through all of us. We gon' all always be products of you. Peace, old man." JaMichael said touching his stone. "Y'all, let's get the fuck out of here. Thank y'all for having this moment with us. For me, it meant a lot."

"For me too." Jahliya agreed.

***

When they got back in the truck, Makaroni turned to JaMichael. "Bruh, why was it important that me and Montana came down here with y'all to do this?"

JaMichael closed the door to his truck, and leaned his back against the seat. Both Jahliya and Montana had rolled away inside of Jahliya's Benz truck already. JaMichael sparked his blunt as Makaroni rolled down the long road that led away from the cemetery. "Man, y'all family, bruh. Me and Jahliya would never brang anybody here to celebrate or visit our parents unless we cared about them. All three of our parents make up what we have been able to accomplish to this day. We will never forget them. You gotta cherish your mother, Makaroni. You never know when life will separate y'all. You feel me?"

Makaroni nodded. "Yeah. I feel you." He rolled for a few moments in silence. JaMichael passed him the blunt and he took it. "I appreciate both of y'all for allowing us to be a part of that though. On some real shit, it was special to me."

"Don't even mention it, homeboy. It's time for you to focus in on this next move anyway. After this, both you and your Potna a be able to progress to the next level."

"Cuz, let's get it."

Chapter 16

The wind howled loudly. It kicked up a bunch of litter that had been carelessly left on the street. Snow fell from the sky in light snowflakes. The night sky seemed darker than usual. Maisey pulled her Plymouth Neon into the back of her duplex, and cut the engine. She gathered up her purse, cellphone and gloves, before opening the driver's door. The burst of air caused her hair to blow in the wind. She pulled her hat down further over her head. After her ears were covered, she traveled to the back of her car, and popped the trunk, going inside of it and taking out the six Walmart plastic grocery bags. "Damn." She muttered as she dropped her car keys to the ground. She crouched down, and tried her best to pick them up without letting go of the bags. After a couple of unsuccessful attempts, she finally submitted to setting the bags down so she could retrieve her keys. She scooped them up, and dropped them inside of one of the grocery bags and stood up.

The wind blew harder. Her left arm was straining by the time she made it to her backdoor. She sat the bags back down. Now she was trying to remember which one of them she had placed her keys inside. She searched through one bag at a time.

Stacy stepped from the side of the house with a mask covering his face. He took a .45 off of his hip, and cocked it. His two Shooters stood behind him, ready for him to give them a command. Stacy sucked his teeth. "Say, Shorty. Ain't you Makaroni mama?"

Maisey looked up at Stacy. As soon as she saw the mask, she backed away. "Hey, look. I don't know what my son did to you, but it ain't got nothing to do with me. Please leave my backyard." She was seconds away from screaming.

Stacy pointed his gun at her. "Look, lady, we just wanna ask you some questions. Come here."

Maisey backed up to the fence of her backyard. "Please, leave me alone. It's cold. I wanna get in the house."

Now Stacy was getting irritated. "Look, bitch. Yo punk ass son and that nigga Stevo smoked a few of my lil' workers down the way. I know it was them 'cause I keep a camera on all if my spots. Plus, one of my lookouts say they saw them niggas run back to Stevo crib. Now you better tell me where they at. Matter fact, bring yo ass here." He lunged forward.

Maisey smacked his gun as hard as she could, making it go off. Then she turned and hopped the fence, taking off running as fast as she could. Having ran track in high school it was like riding a bike to her. She was thankful that she kept herself in shape. She ran into the alley and sped up. When she looked over her shoulder, the trio were just a short distance away. She ran left, and wound up in somebody's backyard. She ran out of it, and to the front of the house. She hopped another fence and ran down the street. "Help me! Help me! Please, help me!" She screamed.

Stacy ran through the gangway and was the first to come out on the street. He saw that Maisey was slowing down. She was running a little less than a jog. He pushed himself to sprint as fast as he could. She tried to look over her shoulder, and tripped over her own feet. She fell face-first. He jumped, and landed on top of her. "Bitch, you had to make this shit difficult, didn't you?"

Maisey fought against him in a panic. She kicked. She clawed. It was of no use. Stacy was too strong. He held her down.

Stacy's Hitta's blue Tahoe pulled up, and slammed on its brakes. He jumped out, and helped to zip tie Maisey's hands and feet. They picked her up and tossed her into the back of the truck.

"Since this bitch wanna fight, I got a trick for her ass." Stacy announced. "Take her to the Trap off of Twenty-fifth and Wells Street. Hurry up." He ordered.

***

Makaroni wiggled his fingers into the leather gloves. He pulled them up his hands. "You ready to handle dis business, Stevo?"

Stevo was gone off of Pink Mollie. His pupils were dilated. He felt like killing something. For some reason he felt incredibly angry. "Man, let's get this shit over with so we can get back to the city. I miss Milwaukee, man. Straight up."

Makaroni didn't really give a fuck about Milwaukee. The only thing he missed about it was his mother Maisey. He was feening to hug her, and to taste some of her soul food. "Aiight, then. The sooner we do what we gotta do, the better."

It was freezing cold outside. Frozen rain dropped from the sky like hail. It was one o'clock in the morning. Makaroni pulled the stolen Chevy three houses down from Geoffrey's. "Bruh say all we gotta do is hit dude bitch ass, and get that money back that he just gave him. Then we hit up Black Haven and air that bitch out, hollering Orange Mound, and it's over with. We are on to the next level."

"I still can't believe we about to go in here and get a million dollars in cash. Then we finna bring that shit right back to JaMichael instead of hopping on the road. Nigga, do you know what we could do with a million dollars?" Stevo asked, wishing that Makaroni could see things his way.

"Hell yea,h I do. That shit gon' come for us. All we gotta do is stay the course. Patience is everything when it comes to the Game." Makaroni reminded him.

143

"No, the fuck it ain't. That's the reason why niggas get in the Game, because they searching for that fast money. That's common sense."

"That might be so, but this ain't our fast money, bruh. It's my cousin's. And since it is, we gotta handle shit on the up and up. That's just how shit gotta play out."

Stevo shook his head. "You know if it was my cousin, we'd be breaking his ass off. But it's good. Let's just handle this business, and do shit yo way."

***

Makaroni took the glass cutter, and cut a circle into Geoffrey's backdoor. He picked the piece of glass out, and placed it on the ground. Then he stuck his arm into the backdoor, and felt around until he found the lock. As soon as he found it, he clicked it open. He looked back at Stevo. "We good."

Stevo nodded. "Aiight, let's go."

Makaroni slowly pushed the door inward. It creaked. The sound of it made his stomach do somersaults. He stepped into the living room. His eyes took a while to adjust to the darkness. When they did, he saw that the living room was junky, and over cluttered. There was a piano to his left, and to his right a pile of clothes that were set to be taken to the cleaners. It smelled like bacon and sweaty feet. The stench was enough to make him gag.

Stevo walked up to him and placed his hand on his shoulder. "Bruh said dude fat ass sleep upstairs. His room is way in the back. Let's go get his ass." Stevo crept up the stairs slow and steady. They felt like they were about to cave inward. He couldn't understand how a man with as much money as Geoffrey had could live like such a slob. When he got to the top stair, he took a deep breath and held it. He was trying to see if he could hear anything but the only thing he heard was the steady ticking of the clock downstairs. He crouched low and stayed as close to the wall as possible, headed directly for Geoffrey's bedroom.

Makaroni checked each room on the way to make sure that there were no other people present. He knew he could never be too sure. When he got to the bathroom door, he heard the toilet flush. That stopped him in his tracks. The carpet felt rough under his Jordan's. He wanted to call out to Stevo but it was too late. Stevo turned the knob to Geoffrey's rooms and rushed inside. Makaroni opened the bathroom door, and pointed his gun.

A heavyset black woman screamed and threw her hands in the air. "Please don't shoot."

Stevo rushed the bed. He could hear grunting and whimpering. He pulled the sheets off of Geoffrey's humping body, and hit him in the back of the head with the barrel of his gun. "Bitch ass nigga, break yo self."

Makaroni came to the doorway, and turned on the light. He had his arm around the heavyset black woman's throat. He flung her to the floor. "Bitch, don't move." He looked to the bed and saw a naked, crying and shaking little girl. He frowned. "What the fuck is going on up in here?" He snapped.

"Please, baby. I couldn't pay my rent, so I had to give him my daughter." The heavyset woman cried.

Stevo threw a sheet over the little girl. He kicked Geoffrey in the jaw. "Sick muthafucka. Where that money at?"

Geoffrey flew backward. His head was bleeding. Blood ran down the back of his neck and into his lower waistband. "I don't know what you're talking about." His legs were open to reveal a Vienna sausage sized penis.

Makaroni took the little girl and led her to the closet. "Stay in here and don't come out. Do you understand me?" He asked.

She nodded. She sat in the closet and wrapped the sheet tighter around her frail body. "What about my mama?"

Makaroni closed the door on her question. He mugged the lady on the floor. "This is what you do to your child? Huh?"

She sniffled. "It was either that or the streets. We didn't have a choice."

Stevo ran across the room and straddled her. He proceeded to beat her senseless with the gun until his arm gave out. The woman yelped, and screamed but it fell on deaf ears. Blood popped up and wet the walls. He kept beating harder and harder. His heavy breathing was loud in the room.

Makaroni didn't have the willpower to stop him. The lady had been bogus. He couldn't understand how anybody could sell their child to a predator like Geoffrey. He kept the fat man at gunpoint. If he moved in the slightest, he wasn't sure if he would've been able to prevent himself from pulling the trigger and killing him on the spot.

When Stevo stood up, he had blood dripping from his gun. The heavyset woman's skull was wide open. There was a puddle under her. "That bitch bogus. Fuck her." He snapped. "Fuck her."

Makaroni pulled up Geoffrey, and sat him in a love seat that was on the side of the bed. It had the kid's clothes on it. This infuriated Makaroni. "Check dis out, homie. We need dat million that JaMichael paid you today."

Geoffrey kept his mouth shut. He should've known not to trust JaMichael. Now that he had signed all of the necessary paperwork to turn over the properties to him, JaMichael was coming back for his cash. Geoffrey felt like a damn fool. He grew angry. He knew he had to play this smart. He'd watched Stevo beat the woman to death. He knew that he was dealing with at least one loose cannon. "Look, I don't have the cash here. I deposited it in my bank account. I do have a substantial amount of cash that I could give you if you allow for me to leave here with my life."

Makaroni grabbed a pillow from the bed. He placed it over Geoffrey's shoulder and pulled the trigger. Geoffrey jumped up from the chair, and hollered out in pain. Stevo swung and cracked his jaw. He fell back to the chair in excruciating pain.

"Okay. Okay. Listen. I don't have all of the money here. I wish I did. But, I can get it tonight. It's at my other house." He lied, not sure himself of what he was trying to accomplish. The stubbornness inside of him made him refuse to give up the money without a hassle.

"Dis mafucka think we playing wit' him." Stevo snapped. He aimed his gun directly at Geoffrey's head. "Where is that million? You got three seconds to tell me, bitch, and I'm starting at two."

"Downstairs, right by the garage door. It's in two white duffel bags. You can count it; it's all there." He swore.

Makaroni left the room. He jogged through the house. When he got downstairs, he found the duffel bags right where Geoffrey said they would be. He knelt, and searched through them. When he saw that both bags were filled with cash he smiled. "I got it, bruh. It's down here."

Stevo nodded. "Good looking, homie." He slammed his gun between Geoffrey's thighs and proceeded to pull the trigger over and over again.

Geoffrey stood up with blood gushing out of his privates. He turned to run and both balls fell to the carpet. He dropped to his knees. Stevo stood over him and popped him twice in the back of the head. "Sick bastard." He grabbed the little girl out of the closet, and they left the house.

**

A masked Makaroni stopped and jumped out of the car with the little girl. He rang the doorbell to the firehouse, and put her down. "Tell them what the scary man was doing to you. Tell them everything. God bless, Shorty." He jumped back into the car. Stevo stormed away from the curb with smoke billowing from the tires.

Chapter 17

It was a day later, and Maisey found herself inside of the dark, dank basement of Stacy's blow Trap. There were big rats that scurried around her feet. A few of them had come to stop and sniff her, before screeching away. Maisey struggled against the binds. She had a red ball inside of her mouth that was used as a gag. She had not eaten in over twelve hours. Her stomach growled. She felt dizzy. She wondered what the men had in store for her. So far, they hadn't done more than have her sit in the dark for hours on end. She'd been offered Checkers restaurant food one time and had declined it.

Stacy made his way down the wooden steps. He jumped off of the last one that was missing a wooden covering, and flipped on the red light so that it lit up the basement. He smiled as he looked across the expanse of the basement, and saw Maisey struggling to break free. "Shorty, ain't no use in you trying to do all of that. You ain't finna break those binds. Yo lil' weak ass ain't strong enough." He stepped up to her, and rubbed the side of her face.

She cringed, and jerked her head away. She mugged him with intense hatred. Sweat slid down the back of her neck. She could tell that the heat had been cranked up to the max. She felt sticky, and irritated.

Stacy laughed. He grabbed a handful of her hair, and yanked her head back. "Aw, so you one of those tough old women, huh?" He yanked on the strands.

Maisey yelped in pain. She could feel her hair coming out at the roots. As much as it hurt, she refused to shed a tear. She said a silent prayer to God in her mind, and kept her composure.

Stacy released his hold. He leaned into her face. "Listen to me. I need to know where yo punk ass son is. He did a few acts on my people that I can't live with. So, I'm finna take this gag out of yo mouth, and you gon' tell me what's good. Aiight?"

Maisey thought his breath smelled like tuna. She wished she could plug her nose to prevent being forced to smell it. She nodded. She was praying that she could find an opening to attack him. She didn't see any of his Goons around. She felt that she could take him one on one. He was only one man.

"Aiight." Stacy grabbed her by the hair, and yanked the ball out of her mouth roughly. "Talk, bitch."

Maisey inhaled a breath of fresh air. She closed her eyes. Her chest began to rise and fall faster and faster as if she were having an asthma attack. She tried to calm down. "My son ain't in town." She rasped.

"Bitch, what?" Stacy grabbed her hair again. It was his go-to move. Whenever the females that he pimped got out of line, he yanked strands of their hair out. Whenever he needed them to tell him the truth when he felt like they were lying, he used the same technique. He knew it was a painful process. They often folded and became submissive. He was sure that Maisey would be the same way.

"I said my son is not in town. He been gone for a while now. I don't know what he did, but can you please forgive him? I am begging you."

Stacy let her go. He stood back, and mugged her. "Bitch, do you know that your son killed three of my homeboys? He kilt three of them, and took some shit that belonged to me. You think it's gon' be that easy for me to just let that go? Huh?"

"What are you planning on doing to my baby?" She asked, eyeing him with increasing anger.

Stacy laughed. "Bitch, when I catch yo son, and his bum ass friend?" He laughed. "I'ma skin them fuck boys. I'ma skin them alive. Then I'ma pour salt all over their wounds until they are screaming from pain. When I feel like I had enough of watching them suffer, that's when I'ma slice their throats from ear to ear." He demonstrated with his finger across his own neck. "What you think about that?"

Maisey looked up at him with a solemn smile on her face. "Lil boy, I think you done seen one too many movies."

Stacy mugged her for a long time, then he busted up laughing. "You think this shit is a game, huh?" He ripped open her blouse, exposing her black lace bra. The brown globes appealed to him under the red light. "Damn, I knew you had some pretty ass titties. Look at them mafuckas." He grabbed a hold of the lace material, and yanked it in two different directions. Her breasts came spilling out.

Maisey closed her eyes. She couldn't believe this was happening to her. "What do you want from me, boy? What?" She hollered.

"Oh, I told you what I wanted. You telling me that he ain't in town, so what we gone do is celebrate each other until he get back in town. How do that sound to you?"

She shook her head. "This ain't right, baby. Please don't do this. Please don't do this to me."

Stacy wasn't trying to hear nothing. He had already made his mind up. He had to have Maisey. It would be the ultimate slap in the face to Makaroni and Stevo. He laughed as he knocked Maisey's chair to the floor. He began ripping her clothes from her body with animalistic hunger.

***

"Dawg, what's up with you? You ain't said a word since yesterday." Makaroni said, looking over at Stevo as they sat in Jahliya's Benz truck that was parked in front of the mansion. It was two days after he had taken care of Geoffrey, and

JaMichael had disappeared. Both men were waiting on him so they could be blessed with the next level of the Game. They expected to take those levels back to Milwaukee where they could set up shop, and start the money train.

"Nigga, I still can't believe that we gave up a million dollars in cash. I feel like a got-damn fool. Straight up."

Makaroni became frustrated immediately. "You still dwelling on that shit?"

Stevo nodded. "Hell yeah, I am. We sitting around here waiting on this nigga to return to hold up his end of the bargain when we had a whole ass million dollars. Nigga, we stick up kids first and foremost. Then Dope Boys. We are stick up kids because we need and crave that fast money. We had the fastest million dollars we probably gon' see in our entire life and we gave that shit back. You lucky I love you, Makaroni. If I didn't, I would've had to slump you and rolled off into the sunset with that money."

Makaroni looked at him from the corners of his eyes. "Fuck you just say?" He felt offended.

"You heard me loud and clear. I didn't stutter. I'm tired of being a bum. Tired of being a worker. Tired of everybody riding foreign around me, and we ain't even got a car. Nigga, I ain't never been nobody's bitch. Ain't no nigga pimping me. Where the fuck is JaMichael?" He snapped. "I want what I am owed! Straight the fuck up."

Makaroni lowered his head. He was still trying to process the part where Stevo said that if he wasn't his guy that he would've slumped him and took the money. He figured that those thoughts must've crossed his mind more than a few times. That angered him. "Bruh, I know you are feeling some type of way right now because my cousin ain't here. But—"

"But nothing, nigga. Ain't no fuckin' buts to it. We handled our business. Now he supposed to be setting us straight.

We done bodied more than a few mafuckas for him. Risked our lives and shit. Yet, this bitch ass nigga ain't nowhere to be found. That's weak ass fuck!" He punched the dashboard.

Makaroni flared his nostrils. "Nigga, you acting like a bitch right now. On everything you making me wanna get at yo chin. But I'ma let you have this lil' temper tantrum."

"Nigga, you acting like a bitch. Fuck you, Makaroni. Fuck you. Fuck Jahliya. And fuck JaMichael."

After the words left his mouth, JaMichael rolled up the driveway inside of a stretch Navigator. He waited until the chauffeur opened his door. Then he stepped out fresh. He was rocking a Givenchy three-piece suit over Balenciaga loafers.

Stevo saw him through the rear-view window. He jumped out of the whip and walked directly up to him. He ignored the two huge bodyguards that were standing behind JaMichael.

JaMichael smiled. "What's good, lil' bruh?"

"You said that you had us as soon as we handled our business. Well, nigga, I want mine. That shit is only fair."

JaMichael nodded. "You got that coming." He looked over his shoulder as a Range Rover truck rolled up the driveway. The Range Rover contained Rubio Flores. Rubio Flores was head of the Sinister Cartel out of Mexico City.

"Yeah, I betta." Stevo was riled up. He was over all of the waiting.

Makaroni walked up and gave JaMichael a half-hug. "What's good, cuz? Where the fuck you been at?"

JaMichael tried his best to keep his composure. He turned around and looked toward Rubio Flores. "When it comes to the Game, you can never progress to the next level without making sure that the Kings over you are okay with it. In this Game, everybody gotta answer to somebody. Now let's go inside, and I'll introduce you to the man that is going to make shit happen for all of us."

***

Ten minutes later JaMichael sat at the head of the long table, while Rubio sat at his right with two short, but deadly, Mexican Shooters behind him. "Awright, now that we are all situated, it's time that I introduce you two to Mr. Rubio Flores. Mr. Flores is head of the newest, and strongest Cartel crew inside of Mexico. The Sinister Cartel. Mr. Flores, this is my lil' cousin Makaroni. Makaroni, this is Mr. Flores. Mr. Flores, him sitting over there's name is Stevo. Stevo, this is Mr. Flores."

"Please. Call me Rubio."

"So, what's good wit' you, Rubio? Don't tell me that we gotta go through another level because he done already took us through a bunch of bullshit already. It's time for us to get money. If you ain't finna talk about that, then this conversation is over."

Makaroni was embarrassed. "Excuse my friend here. He ain't slept in a few days. We been grinding." He shot daggers at Stevo.

Stevo sucked his teeth. "Yeah, whatever."

Rubio eyed both of them with disdain. "Perhaps you could pick two better men to invade the Midwest with such a strong product. These two seem to have their affairs out of order."

JaMichael mugged Stevo. "Mr. Flores, I gave you my word. These two are worthy of your blessing. All I ask is that you give them a chance on the strength of me."

Rubio nodded. "Very well." He took a deep breath, and slowly blew it out. "You get two chances with me. Two chances, and one warning. The first warning is to let you know what you have done wrong. It's also your clue to know that I am on to you, and for you to get your shit together. I will not hesitate to wipe you off of the face of this God forsaken planet. I mean that. There is nowhere you can run, and nowhere you can hide. If you come under me, you are taking an oath that says I own you until I am done with you and your services. Do both of you understand this?"

Stevo looked over to Makaroni. "What do you mean by you own us?"

Rubio felt his temper flaring. "I speak direct language. No emphasis. No beating around the bush. Plain!"

Makaroni held up his hand. "We understand, and we agree. Right, Stevo?"

"Yeah, right."

Rubio continued to look them over for a full minute. He was unsure about the men that sat before him. JaMichael had proven to be a cash cow to his Sinister Cartel. He experienced very few problems with JaMichael. His word had also been good. He didn't think he would put his word on two idiots that could cost him his life. He had to give JaMichael the benefit of the doubt. "Okay then." He nodded at JaMichael.

JaMichael grabbed the briefcase that was on the side of him. He placed it on top of the table, and clicked it open. He took out a metal pan, and a brick of the Rebirth. He sat the Rebirth on top of the metal pan. "This is the Rebirth. My father's legacy. Rubio has taken the ingredients of the Rebirth and found a way to make them stronger. One brick of the Rebirth can be broken down to make four regular bricks of a high potency heroin. This product is dangerous, and it is so addictive that you will literally own whoever comes into use of this product. They will be at your mercy. However, if you are not careful, the power that you have over people because of this drug will go to your head. You will become arrogant. Your addicts will kill you over this product. You have to be smart. Once a person uses the Rebirth, they will never be able to stop using it as long as they can get their hands on it. Do you two understand this?"

Makaroni and Stevo nodded in unison. They eyed the product with newfound fascination. Neither could believe what they were hearing was the truth. But JaMichael had not told them one lie.

"Secondly. You will not use this product yourselves. If I am to find out that you are using this supply of The Rebirth, I will terminate you, and take your life immediately. Do you understand that?" Rubio asked.

"Yep." Stevo agreed.

"We don't fuck wit' nothing but bud anyway." Makaroni offered.

"That's good. Now, usually we invade the Midwest through the dumping post of Chicago, Illinois. But since you two will be the catalyst for the Rebirth in the Midwest, we will begin with Milwaukee. We will allow for you to set up and distribute as you see fit. We will assist in your property acquiring, and expansion. You will answer first to JaMichael, and then to me. I am a very busy man. You will be given quotas based off of your city, and the regions we invade. We will work from Milwaukee down to Chicago. We will invade, and infect the inner cities first. That is always the easiest route to take. The opposition doesn't care how much you infect the urban areas. It doesn't become a problem until you venture us into the suburbs. There is a lot of data that goes with everything that we are pursuing, but you can see how JaMichael is living. That should prove to you that the system works." He sat back, and looked over to JaMichael. "Is there anything else that you would like to say?"

JaMichael nodded. "Within every level of the Game there is a play that is called divide and conquer. In order for your dollars to add up as fast as you would like them to, you must divide your rivals. You can have a thousand rivals or enemies. If you can divide them, and place them against each other, you can conquer them. So, I say that to say just because you two will be getting large amounts of cash now, it doesn't mean that you will be able to put your guns down. That murder shit is still in effect. Especially since you are looking to take over a new city. Understand that there."

Rubio stood up, and adjusted his expensive suit. He was five feet five inches tall. He had dark brown hair, and sharp brown eyes. "Seeing as I have said my peace, it's best that I depart. I wish you men the best." He shook all three of their hands before he and his henchmen left the property.

"Well, boys, tonight I'ma get y'all right. As of this moment, consider yourselves elevated to level two of the Game."

Ghost

Chapter 18

It was Sunday. Two days after Makaroni and Stevo had been elevated to the second stage of the Game, Makaroni sat across from Jahliya inside of Tracy's House of Barbecue. It was a nice restaurant located in the more upscale area of North Memphis. They had just been given their dishes.

Jahliya placed a napkin on her lap, and scooted forward. She picked up her silverware and began to cut into her Shoulder Rib dinner. "So, how have you liked it down here, Mack?"

Makaroni broke apart his ribs, and poured some of Tracy's secret barbecue sauce on it. He shrugged. "I really didn't get a chance to enjoy myself down here. It was straight business the whole time, which was cool, but it's all good."

Jahliya finished chewing the savory piece of pork that she was chewing on. The special sauce had her taste buds firing on all cylinders. She closed her eyes until she swallowed the last piece. When she opened them, she was mugging her plate as if she were mad at how good the food was. "Damn, that girl be putting her foot down." She announced. She looked over at Makaroni. "Well, you mean to tell me that you didn't enjoy JaMichael's birthday and welcome home bash?" She looked him over to see what his response was going to be. She popped another piece of meat into her mouth, still in disbelief because of its taste.

"I mean, I really ain't attend it like that. But like I said, it's good. We came down here on a mission. We fulfilled that mission. Now it's time to go back up here to Milwaukee and handle our business. It ain't more excuses for our financial struggles. You feel me?"

Jahliya put her fork down, and gave him all of her attention. "You wanna know something?"

"What's that?" Makaroni ate a piece of his barbecued rib. "Damn, she snapped." He eyed the rest of his rib hungrily.

"I know for a fact that you are going to be a Boss." She rested her chin on her hand.

"Oh, yeah? How do you know that?"

"Because you come from nothing just like me and Ja-Michael. You got that same look in your eyes that he had when he was your age, and going through the same things that you are right now. Ever since he got that push, he ain't looked back since. That's how I know. I mean, that and we have the same bloodline."

Makaroni stared at her. He had never taken the time out to really look Jahliya over, but now that he was, he had to admit that she was a bad bitch. She was gorgeous. With her almond shaped eyes. Her smooth caramel skin. Her Barbie doll like feature, and natural hair. Her body was even better. He couldn't believe that she was as fine as she was. She reminded him of a thicker version of Gabrielle Union-Wade. "Well, I ain't got no room to lose. I gotta make shit happen. That's what I'm finna do." He was confident. Focused. He knew that he was being given the opportunity that most starving kids in Chicago and Milwaukee never got. Not just those places, but ghettos all over the globe. But now he was in. He was adamant about making the best of his opportunity.

Jahliya eyed him hungrily. There was no way that she was about to allow for him to go back to Milwaukee without her giving him some pussy. "I know that you really didn't get a chance to enjoy Memphis like you were supposed to, so how about you and I kick it for a few days straight uninterrupted? What do you think about that?"

Makaroni felt his dick twitch. He eyed her breasts. Then his focus was back on her gorgeous face. He couldn't fathom the thoughts that were really taking place in her mind. "I would love to kick it with you. What about Stevo though?"

Jahliya frowned. "N'all, just me and you. Gon' head and eat up. We finna cruise through the city. I got a lil' spot that I want us to hit up. I promise you gon' love it."

"Love it?" Makaroni raised an eyebrow. "You sure you wanna make that promise?"

She smiled. Both dimples appeared on her cheeks. "Yeah, I'm willing to promise you that." She looked into his eyes. Her clit poked between her sex lips and began to throb. She shifted uncomfortably.

"Aiight den, we on."

She crossed her thick thighs, and proceeded to eat her food.

***

Maisey opened her eyes, and took a huge deep breath as if she had been under water for way too long and was just now reaching the surface. She sat up on the dirty mattress that had been placed on the floor of one of the locked rooms inside of Stacy's Trap house. There was a severe stinging between her thighs. Her privates hurt. Both of them. Stacy had taken to screwing her for hours on end for the last few days. He'd only slowed for her to shower one time during the sessions. She felt sick. She felt disgusted. She felt powerless. She felt like she wanted to kill him. She rubbed her temples. Her head was pounding worse than ever. She eased out of the bed, and stood naked on the side of it.

The room was small. There was nothing but a dirty mattress. Two sheets. A bed pan. Two boxes of pizza, and a two-liter bottle of Sprite present inside of it. She flipped on the light, and looked around.

The windowed been boarded up by Stacy. She didn't know if it had bars on it or not. The door to the room was locked from the outside. She was unsure of his many guards he had on duty to make sure that she didn't escape, but she was sure that he had at least two. She sat back on the bed lost in her own thoughts. She wondered if her children had come looking for her yet. At the very least, she prayed that they had become suspicious. She wondered if Cassidy or Seth had contacted Makaroni or Montana. Surely, they were thrown off at the fact that she had not been home in days. Weren't they? She wondered. She heard a rambling at the door. She scooted as far away from the door as she could.

Stacy took the locks off of the door, and stepped inside of the room. He had a change of clothes, and a bag of Jake's Corn Beef in his hands. He closed the door behind him. "Hey, baby, how you feeling?" He laughed.

Maisey eyed him with intense hatred. "Don't call me your baby. When are you going to let me out of here?" She said with her voice cracking up.

He sat the bag of food on the ground, and took his gun out. He cocked it. "What did I tell you about asking me that shit? Huh? Didn't I tell you that I would release yo ass when I was ready to release you? Huh?"

Maisey ignored his questions. "When it's all said and done, you are going to beg me to stop my son from torturing you. I don't give a fuck what you got up your sleeve. When it is all said and done, you will reap what you have sown. Trust me on this."

Stacy snatched her up by her throat and slung her into the wall. "When you get to talking like that, it only pisses me off." He ripped the covers from her and threw her to the bed. He aimed his gun. "Open them mafuckin' thighs and let me see that pussy?"

Maisey scooted back to the wall. "Let me out of here. Please."

"Shorty, if you thinking I'm playing wit' you, you're about to find out the real. Now open them mafuckin' thighs, and let me see that pussy." Stacy had become obsessed with degrading Maisey. Second to that, her body drove him crazy. Because of his kingpin status, women all over Milwaukee broke their necks to sleep with him. Maisey hated his guts. That drove him crazy. He was obsessed with what he couldn't have. What he wasn't supposed to have. He had always been that way.

Maisey closed her eyes and opened her thighs. Her pussy popped out at him. She refused to look him in the eyes. She felt so low.

"Dat's what I'm talking about. Now play wit' that mafucka while I watch." He unbuckled his belt. Pulled his dick out.

Maisey felt like crying. Instead of allowing for him to see her tears, she took a deep breath. She imagined that she was in the room of her home all alone.

"Fuck taking you so long?" He pointed the .45 at her with the hammer cocked.

She slid her fingers into her pussy, and rubbed them up and down the slit. She needed to find his weakness. She needed to find a way to penetrate him. Needed to seize the opportunity to escape when it presented itself. She closed her eyes, and then opened them when she heard him groan.

Stacy's eyes were pinned right on Maisey's gap. "Damn, you strapped down there. I can fuck you a hundred times a day and never get tired." He stroked his piece faster. "Open it up for me."

She spread the lips. Her pink exposed. She watched him shiver. He moved forward toward the bed. Knelt between her thighs with the gun still in his hand. "I gotta hit this pussy again. I just got to." He kept the .45 in his right hand while he lined himself up with his left. With one thrust he sank into her hotness. Then he was plunging, stroking like a horny dog.

Tears ran down Maisey's cheeks. She placed her hands on his chest, ready to push him off of her, but she feared what he would do if she did, so she accepted everything that he was doing to her.

"Uh. Uh. Uh. Uh." He felt her womb tugging at him on its own accord. He sucked her neck, and plunged deeper and deeper. "I'ma do Montana the same way. Uh. Uh. Uh. Montana gon'... Uh. Uh. Get this. Same treatment!" He dove deep, and started to cum inside of her for the fifteenth time. He growled, and laid flat out.

Maisey felt the seed squirting inside of her, and she lost it. She pulled him by the dreads and bit a chunk out of his face. She spit it out. Then she latched on again. She had a mouth full of his cheek.

Stacy hollered as loud as he could. He tried to remove her with both hands; absentmindedly he placed the gun in the floor to do so. "Bitch, get off of me!"

Maisey brought her knee up and slammed it into his testicles as hard as she could. He fell on top of her, winching in pain. She bit him again. Rolled him off of her, and ran toward the door that she was sure he had neglected to lock. She threw it wide open, and took off running down the hallway. She ran to the kitchen. There were two young females inside of it, cooking up two kilos of coke. She ran past them directly to the backdoor. She threw it open, and ran off into the night, running for her life.

Stacy staggered into the hallway with blood running down his face. There was a massive hole. His cheek bone underneath was clearly visible. "That bitch. Where did that bitch go?" He asked the girls in the kitchen. They simply pointed toward the open backdoor. He cursed. "The one time I got my security somewhere else, this bitch pull this shit!" He dropped to his knees. "One of you hoez gotta drive me to the hospital. Hurry up."

***

Jahliya sat back and watched as Roxy gave Makaroni a slow, sensual lap dance. Roxy was one of the best strippers in her club. Not only was she the main attraction but she was killing things on the adult entertainment side. She was dark brown with a flawless face, and sized forty-five ass. She could tell that Makaroni was getting the ride of his life over his clothes. She felt a bit jealous. "How are you feeling over there, Makaroni?"

She had brought him to her famous strip club. Introduced him to a few of the money-making dancers. He had personally chosen Roxy to take back to the private room. They had been all over each other ever since. Avant crooned from the speakers. Roxy slow-wind facing him. Her pussy rubbed against his piece. "You better answer her."

Makaroni was lost for a minute. He had Roxy kissing all over his neck. His big hands gripped her ass. "Dis what's really good, cuz. What's it gon' take for me to get a room wit' Shorty though? I ain't trying to have this end here."

Roxy snickered. "That's my manager right there. All she gotta do is give me the word and I'm gone."

Jahliya stood up with a bottle of Ace of Spaces in her hand. "N'all, bitch, get up out of here for a minute. Let me holler at my lil' cousin for a second."

Roxy was stunned. "Girl, you fa real?"

Jahliya snapped her fingers. "Yeah, bitch. Get yo ass up and out. Don't make me say it again."

Roxy stood up, and gathered her things. She couldn't understand why Jahliya was acting so bogus toward her. "Awright, well I guess I'll holler at you another time,

Makaroni. If you wanna get up with me, just hit me up on Facebook." She left the room.

Jahliya slammed the door and locked it. She took a swallow from her bottle of champagne. "That bitch so damn thirsty. Ugh." She looked over to Makaroni. He seemed angry to her. "What? You salty because I put her ass out a somethin'?"

Makaroni eyed how her skirt was fitting her thighs. Jahliya was small up top, but after you crossed the equator of her waist, she was as thick as gumbo before you stirred it. His eyes roamed all over her body. "N'all, dat bitch work for you. She forced to do what you say do. It is what it is."

Jahliya sighed. "I guess I ruined yo night out wit' me, huh?"

Makaroni shrugged. "It's cool. I'm ready to get back to Milwaukee anyway."

Jahliya sucked on her bottom lip. "I ain't finna put a damper on your spirits, and let you leave Memphis with me being the reason that your last night out was garbage. N'all, I got other plans than that." She licked her lips.

"I'm saying. Shorty was giving me a cold ass lap dance. Probably the best one I done ever had in my life. How you finna compete wit' that? I mean, unless you finna call her ass back in here."

"N'all, fuck that bitch." She waved Roxy off. "Besides, I taught her everything that she know."

Makaroni dusted off his lap. "So, what you saying then?"

Jahliya felt her clit throb. She sat her bottle of champagne on the table. "If you insisting what I think you is, I'm 'bout that, Playboy. You forget that I got that same shit running through my veins that you do."

Makaroni opened his pants, and pulled them down so that his boxers were exposed. He began to take his lowers off.

"Den get yo thick ass over here and show me what this Memphis shit like."

Ghost

Chapter 19

Trey Songz crooned through the speakers while Jahliya took one last sip from her champagne. She sat the bottle back down, and stepped in front of Makaroni. He ran his hands all over her caramel thighs. She stepped forward a bit more. His hand slipped under her skirt, and between her gap. The fingers rubbed all over her panty-covered pussy. Jahliya moaned. "Mmm. Mack." She closed her eyes, and spaced her feet.

Makaroni pulled her panties down her thighs. Past her knees, and off. She stepped out of them, and turned her back to him. He leaned forward and kissed her right on her left ass cheek, and then the right. He kneaded her soft globes like dough. He opened the cheeks, and licked around her crinkle. His tongue swiped at her pussy.

"Mmm. Boy, you so nasty. You know this ain't right." She swatted him away. Then she lowered herself into his lap, sitting on his hot skin. She could feel his dick poking up against her groove.

Makaroni sucked on the back of her neck. His tongue trailed all the way around until he bit into the thick vein on her left side. "Cuz, I want some of this pussy bad. Every time you walk across me, I feel my nature calling out for you. I don't know what it is. But ever since I smelled your scent it's been like that." He sucked and bit all over her neck, gripping her breasts.

Jahliya moaned. "It's yo blood, Makaroni. You can't help it. Neither can I." She began to slow grind in his lap. Her ass cheeks trapped his pole. She rode it slowly. Her juices leaked out of her slit, drenching him. She wanted to fuck him so bad. "Mmm. Baby. You know I got cameras in every bedroom of my house, right?"

Makaroni pulled her hard nipples. He slid his hand in front of her, and found her sex lips. She was dripping wet. "And? What that got to do wit' what we doing?" He hissed. He sucked harder on her neck.

She moaned. "I saw you fucking her, Makaroni. I watched you dick Montana down while we were having JaMichael's party. I didn't see you down there. I was wondering what was going on with you, so I tuned into the camera in your room just as Montana walked into it, and I saw y'all. I knew me and JaMichael wasn't the only one that got down like that in this family."

Makaroni stopped sucking, caught off guard. His dick got to jumping up and down like crazy. He couldn't believe his ears. "So you and cuz done fucked before?"

She nodded. "Yeah." She flipped around and straddled his waist. Her short skirt rose on to her lower back. Makaroni's piece rested up against her stomach. She could feel it beating like crazy against her. It felt like a hot, throbbing cucumber that had been left in the microwave too long. "I wanna fuck you, Makaroni. I wanna fuck you right here and right now. But while we're doing it, I need you to talk that shit to me." She stood up just a tad, and took a hold of his dick, before she eased down on it. She sank, then eased back off of it, leaving it shiny and sticky. "Damn, you got a lot of meat."

Makaroni felt more horny than he had ever felt. He began to shake. He could still imagine the tightness of Jahliya's womb. He wanted to be back in there. "Jahliya, if you don't sit back on this mafucka, I'm finna take this pussy from you. I ain't playing either."

Jahliya felt a volt of electricity shoot through her clitoris. She stood up with her skirt around her waist. She rubbed her sex lips in his face. "You know what? We can't do this. We family, Makaroni. That ain't what family do." She pulled her skirt down, and walked away from him.

Makaroni didn't let her get more than ten steps. He jumped up, and pushed her face-first into the wall of the private room. He got behind her, and yanked her skirt up. She attempted to fight away from him. He kicked her feet apart, and found her slit. Once there, he placed two fingers inside of her and ran them in and out of her at full speed.

Jahliya's mouth was wide open. She slobbered a bit. Her clit was as big as it had ever been. "Unn. Unn. Unn. Cuz. Please."

Makaroni removed his fingers quickly. They were dripping with her juices. He replaced the digits with his piece. He grabbed her hips and slammed into her body. Her womb was tight, and wet. The heat was unimaginable. He backed up so he could bend her thick ass over. As soon as she was into position, he stroked her as if his life depended on it. "Fuck. Fuck. Jahliya. Shit, cuz."

Jahliya bounced back over and over into his lap. The harder she slammed backwards the deeper he sank into her treasures. Her sex lips sucked at him greedily. "Fuck. Me. Like. You. Do. Montana. Oh! Shit. Cuz!" She groaned.

Makaroni was in a zone. He couldn't take his eyes off of their connected parts. First Montana, now he was fucking Jahliya. He didn't know what was wrong with him. Why all of the sudden he was craving the off-limits women around him, but he had to admit that their pussies were the best that he'd ever felt before. Jahliya's even smelled intoxicating to him. Every time he reminded himself of their relation, it sent shock waves throughout his body.

Jahliya slammed back into him, and held his thighs to keep him as deep as she could while she came, screaming at the top of her lungs. "Shit. Shit. Shit." She whimpered.

Makaroni pulled out, and picked her up. She wrapped her thick thighs around him. He carried her to the wall and steadied her against it. Then he was tossing her up and down, faster and faster. Her weight felt good to him. *There was nothing like fucking a thick woman*, he thought. He needed that meat. Needed a woman with some flesh on her bones.

Jahliya hopped up and down. She felt Makaroni's dick reaching her deepest levels. His head knocked at her G spot over and over. She licked the side of his face, and came shivering.

Makaroni fell to the ground with her. His hips kept pumping at full speed. The noise coming from in between their thighs resonated in the room. He pulled all the way back, only to slam forward again. His pace was fast. All gas no brakes. He felt her walls sucking at him. He pushed her knees to her shoulders and dug her out with no remorse. "You a boss bitch? You a boss bitch? Huh, cuz?"

The dick was so good that tears ran down Jahliya's cheeks. Her mouth was wide open while she whimpered. Another orgasm rocked her body, and sent her into convulsions. She dug her nails into his back, and scratched. "Uhhhh, Makaroni!"

Makaroni flipped her over, and pulled her knee to her right rib. He laid her on her side, and fucked her with no mercy until he couldn't hold back any longer. "Jahliya! Baby. Where you want it?" He kept clapping, harder. Faster. "Where you want it?"

Her eyes rolled into the back of her head. Love crossed her mind. She finally knew that it was true for a woman to fall in love after a good fucking. She shivered as if she was freezing.

"Jahliya!"

"In me, Makaroni. Cum in me." She whimpered. She needed to feel it.

Makaroni flipped her back onto her back. He forced her knees to her chest again, and came jerking into her. He felt like he was peeing. He kept cuming and cuming. "Fuck."

Jahliya pushed him off of her, and took a hold of his tool. She slid it into her mouth. She could taste her juices mixed with his. His seed stained her tongue. She swallowed more if it. Pumping it up and down to get as much out of it as she could. Then she was straddling him, and sucking all over his chest. "You did that, Mack. You did that."

Makaroni laid back, breathing heavily while she made love to his body with her mouth.

***

When they got back to the mansion, Jahliya cut the engine to the Benz, and sat without getting out of the car. She looked over at him in the darkness. "Lil cuz, you did yo thang. I ain't even gon' lie."

Makaroni laughed. "You got a snapper on you. I can't believe we did that though." He had all sorts of images going through his head of what they had just done.

"Look, Makaroni, I know it ain't no big deal to you, or then again maybe it is. Either way, I want you to keep what we did between us. Don't be telling Stevo. Definitely don't tell Montana. It's only a matter of time before she get to developing feelings for you, as weird as that may seem. I know, it happened to me with JaMichael." She lowered her head.

"Cuz, you got my word. You ain't gon' have to worry about that. I know how to keep shit to myself. Besides, I ain't tryna have that be the last time I hit this pussy." He slid his hand between her thighs, and rubbed her there. She had neglected to put her panties back on. Her folds were still slippery. Light traces of his cum were all over the lips.

Jahliya closed her eyes and allowed for him to play with her. "It won't be. I'ma come scoop you up and take you on a few trips with me. You know, show you how Boss Bitches do shit. I still don't know what yo head game like, but I'm gon' have to find out about that."

He laughed. She was dead serious. There was an awkward silence inside of the car. The moon shone bright in the night sky. Because she had cut the ignition, it had gotten a bit chilly inside of the vehicle.

"Before we go, Makaroni, I just wanna warn you about the deal you just made with Rubio Flores. Don't break it. If you even look like you are going to go against his wishes, he will annihilate you, and all of our family out there where you are. He is a cold bastard. I don't even think he likes Black folk. I think he just tolerates us because we are cash cows when it comes to the dope trade. That sucks, but I feel it's the truth." She gripped his thigh. "You are about to find out that just because you have money, your problems will not stop. They will only increase tenfold. I have been more miserable with all of this money than I was before we had it. I know that may be hard to believe, but you will see." She kissed him on the cheek. The heat from his skin made her feel almost sexual again. She flashed backe to him pushing her knees to her chest while he pounded her out. She twitched. She felt that she could cum all over again. "Also, watch yo closest friends. Money will turn the best of friends into enemies. These are just jewels that I think you deserve to hear."

Makaroni nodded in the moonlight as it shone through the windshield. "Well, I appreciate this, Jahliya. I just want you to know that I won't take none of this shit lightly. I'm finna be on my business. All of yo jewels that you just dropped, and all of the ones that you will drop, will be worn around my heart. You got my word on that."

She smiled. "Last kiss before we go into the house?"

"Kissing Cousins, huh?" He laughed.

"I guess so." She leaned into him, and they made out loudly for ten minutes straight. By the time they broke apart, they were ready to go at it again.

Ghost

Chapter 20

That night, JaMichael woke Makaroni up at three o'clock in the morning with an assault rifle in his hand. He was breathing hard. He had a mug on his face. "Say, lil' cuz, I need you to roll out to Orange Mound wit' me so we can holler at these Duffel Bag Cartel niggas. They acting like they don't wanna fall in line. But I got a plan for all of that." He slammed a magazine into his Choppah, and cocked it.

Stevo stepped beside him with a grim look on his face. "Mack, get yo ass up so we can go over here and holler at these niggas. JaMichael say that if we ride wit' him tonight that he'll give us ten gees a piece and that it ain't got nothin' to do wit' that Rebirth that we leaving wit'."

"Yeah, lil' homie, I know ten bands ain't a whole lot of money but it's somethin'. Besides, I don't think we gon' have to do much anyway. But in case we do, I know for sure I'll have two Hittas beside me."

Makaroni sat on the edge of the bed. He was more tired than he had ever been before. Jahliya had really worn him out. "Damn, when y'all trying to do all of this?" He yawned.

"Right now. We need to holler at Phoenix n'em like ASAP. That nigga just heard that I've bought up the main property in the Orange Mound where he and his Duffel Bag Cartel crew are operating, and he's insisting that he and I meet face to face to determine how shit is about to go down from here on out. I don't like Phoenix. That nigga is real shysty to me. I don't care if we share the same blood or not."

"Wait, you saying that this nigga is supposed to be some kin to us?" Makaroni asked, before yawning again.

"Yeah, he family. Real distant though. Like a third cousin a somethin'. Anyways, fuck that fool. When it comes to the money, all that family shit is out of the window. Blood don't fund my lifestyle. Nor will it make sure that my sister Jahliya continues to get to live like a Queen. If Phoenix wanna play games wit' me, I'ma buss his brain. That's how that's going to go."

"Shid, I don't care about none of that. All I care about is that five gees and getting back to Milwaukee. I say we go over here and holler at these niggas like ASAP, so I can get my paper. We leaving Memphis tomorrow anyway, so fuck what happens tonight."

"Aiight, that's cool. I need y'all to give me a few minutes to wake up. I'll meet y'all downstairs in like twenty. Bet."

"Bet, lil' cuz. I'm finna catch me a snack anyway." Ja-Michael held his assault rifle up against his shoulder and walked out of the room in his Army fatigues.

Makaroni stood up, and stretched his arms over his head. "Damn." He yawned again. "Ain't no way I could live down here. It's always some bullshit popping off."

Montana stepped into the room. "Boy, the last time I checked in here, you were snoring. What the hell are you doing up right now?" She asked hugging him.

He wrapped his arms around her body, and squeezed her booty. She wore a short night gown that did very little to shield her lowers. "Stevo and JaMichael just woke me. We gotta ride out to Orange Mound so we can handle some business with a crew called the Duffel Bag Cartel. You ever heard of them?" He asked.

She nodded. "Yeah. That's a crew headed by Phoenix Stevens. He's our distant cousin, but him and JaMichael don't really see eye to eye because of Jahliya."

"Because of Jahliya? What she got to do wit' it?"

"That fool JaMichael is very overprotective of her like you are about me. Phoenix is some type of way. He be at Jahliya like she the finest Queen on earth. I mean, I'm not saying that she ain't, but he just overdo it. Second to that, Phoenix had a right-hand man called Mikey. Jahliya was rumored to have hit his ass for a few bricks back in the day. Because Jahliya was Phoenix's blood, he rolled with Jahliya over Mikey. They went to war. Mikey moved out to White Haven; the locals call it Black Haven. When he moved out to Black Haven, he mounted up a bunch of troops and they rode beside him and went to war with Phoenix and his Duffel Bag Cartel crew over in Orange Mound. They had that gunplay, and Mikey wound up on the losing end of that battle. Long story short, Orange Mound and Black Haven been warring ever since. When they war though, JaMichael make money. He supplying both sides because don't nobody else wanna deal with the dealers down there that are stuck in the middle of a warzone."

Makaroni rubbed his chin hairs. "Dat's why that nigga had us do what we did. Okay. Now it make sense. Who supposed to be calling shots for Black Haven?"

"Some young dude named Smoke. He used to be down with the Duffel Bag Cartel until he crossed Phoenix." She sighed. "Yeah, Memphis is crazy. That's why we gotta get the fuck out of here."

Makaroni was frozen in place. He felt like he was being used. He didn't understand what JaMichael had up his sleeve, but he knew it had to be something that benefitted him.

"That ain't the reason why I came in here a few times to see if you were woke though. It's mama. I think something ain't right with her because she ain't responded to none of my Facebook messages. That ain't like her. She usually gets back to me right away." Montana felt uneasy.

"Man, you know how mama is when it comes to that social media shit. Sometimes she wit' it, and other times she ain't. She's cooky like that."

"N'all, Mack. I feel it in my soul. Something ain't right. She ain't answering her phone either."

Stevo knocked on the door. "Fuck taking you so long, Makaroni? We gotta holler at these niggas so we can get on back. Time is money, bruh."

"Yeah, aiight, Stevo. Here I come!" Makaroni hollered.

Montana stepped into his face. "What should we do, big bruh? I'm worried about her."

He hugged her to his body. "Call Cassidy. Call Seth. See if they heard from her. Keep hitting her up on social media too. After I handle this business tonight, we gon' bounce out of Memphis tomorrow and go back home to make sure she straight. Besides, we got some work to put in there anyway. Your brother about to come up major, lil' sis. Mark those words."

"I believe you. Just be careful tonight. Can you do that for me?" She wrapped her arm around his neck, and looked into his eyes.

"I got you. You already know I do."

She stepped forward and kissed him ever so tenderly. Their lip smacking was loud in the room. She breathed heavily. She felt like she was melting in his arms.

Makaroni backed up. His dick was hard. It hurt. "Aiight, sis, go handle that business. I'll see you inna few hours."

She nodded. "Be safe. Please, Mack."

***

JaMichael pulled the black Excursion into the lot of the Orange Mound apartments. He parked the big truck directly in the center of the complex parking lot. Threw it in park, and loaded his hand pistols into his holsters. "I'm letting you niggas know right now that if Phoenix get to talking out the side of his neck, I'm slumping his bitch ass right then and there. I need for y'all to have my back. You can't trust these Duffel Bag Cartel niggas. They shysty."

Makaroni pulled his shirt down over his Teflon vest. He had a .45 in the small of his back, and a Glock in his waistband. He was ready for action. "Look, before you get to shooting and all of that, you need to give us a signal. That way we don't get caught off guard."

"Yeah, we don't know how these niggas get down out here, but you do. So, if you feeling like you about to get on that killa shit, you need to smack the table. Wink ya' eye a something." Stevo added.

"Aiight. If I stand up and say you mafuckas don't think fat meat greasy, that a be y'all cue to let them shots rang out with no remorse. Y'all got that?"

"Yeah." Makaroni cocked his Glock.

"Bet those." Stevo felt his adrenalin pumping.

"Aiight, I'ma go and let this nigga know that I'm here. Y'all chill for a minute. I'ma wave y'all over when it's good." He jumped out of the truck and jogged up to the building. They watched him go inside of it after knocking for a few seconds.

"Say, Stevo, I been meaning to ask you somethin' since we left Milwaukee. It's completely random but I still want you to answer the question. Awright."

"Yeah, nigga, what's up?" Stevo kept looking out of the windshield to see when JaMichael would come back to give them the signal.

"Dawg, I always wanted to know what your mother did to you to make you feel the way that you do toward her. Like, why do you hate her so much?"

Stevo was taken completely off guard. "Nigga, we out here ready to go to war with some clowns that we don't even know? We far away from home. You telling me that's what's on your brain?" He felt himself becoming heated.

"Dawg, I just wanna know. I been wanting to ask you that my whole life. I just never got up the nerve to ask it."

Stevo was hoping that JaMichael came out so he wouldn't have to dive into his personal life, but he didn't see him. "Dawg, what's it to you?"

"I just wanna know, bruh. You my Day One. You know everything about me. That's just a little bit of information that I don't know about you."

"Yeah, well, maybe you don't need to know. You ever thought about that shit? Huh? Have you?"

Makaroni kept his silence. He loved his right hand. He could tell that there was something going on with Stevo underneath the surface. He wanted to find out before they got back to Milwaukee.

"Dawg, my mother sold my sister away to a white family in West Allis." Stevo blurted.

"What?" That was a response that Makaroni wasn't expecting.

"Yeah, she was pregnant with her when we first got up here from Chicago. She wasn't pregnant by my father either. She was pregnant by her high school boyfriend. Some nigga named Neyo. When we got up here to Milwaukee, shit was real hard for us. She could barely afford to feed me. We were living from house to house. She never had enough money to do nothing. Well, two months before she had my sister, one of the landlords offered her a hundred thousand dollars for the female child in her stomach. She didn't flinch. My father didn't want her to have the baby anyway because he knew it wasn't his. Plus, he was fuckin' wit' them drugs real tough back then anyway. But yeah, she sold my sister. The same dude she sold my sister to wound up getting locked up for a bunch of rapes and shit down the road. I can only imagine what he did to her. Even though I never met my sister, I love her. I love her to this day, and I hate my mother because of what she did. I have Seth bitch ass too. That punk ain't no father of mine." He clenched his jaw. "I'll never forgive her, Makaroni. Never. I'ma find my sister too. One of these days I really am."

"Do you even know her name?" Makaroni felt horrible for his homie. He got to imagining what life would've been like if he would've never known Montana. The feeling was enough to make him sick.

"Jada. That's all I know. I don't know her last name or nothing, but Cassidy do."

Makaroni nodded. He rested his hand on Stevo's shoulder. "I appreciate you going there with me, dawg. If you ever wanna find her, I'm wit' you."

"Appreciate that, homie. Soon I am. We gotta get our money right first. Then I'm going to find my lil' sister. That's my word."

"Cool." Makaroni rubber-necked to scan the area. "Man, JaMichael sho' taking a long ass time." His phone vibrated. He took it off of his hip. There was a text from Montana: *Mack, we gotta get back home. They just found mama. She messed up real bad. Life threatening injuries. Call me. ASAP.* Makaroni's stomach dropped.

"Fuck wrong wit' you?" Stevo asked.

Before he could answer the question, two black vans pulled up in back of the Excursion, boxing it in. Ten men jumped out with masks on their faces, and guns in their hands. They surrounded their truck. Phoenix ran around to the front of the Excursion and aimed an assault rifle at the windshield. His red beam lasered into the darkness, searching for a target. "Y'all got three seconds to come up out of that truck or we finna blow this bitch up. This is yo final warning!" He hollered.

To Be Continued...
Drug Lords 2
Coming Soon

Submission Guideline

Submit the first three chapters of your completed manuscript to <u>ldpsubmissions@gmail.com</u>, subject line: Your book's title. The manuscript must be in a .doc file and sent as an attachment. Document should be in Times New Roman, double spaced and in size 12 font. Also, provide your synopsis and full contact information. If sending multiple submissions, they must each be in a separate email.

Have a story but no way to send it electronically? You can still submit to LDP/Ca$h Presents. Send in the first three chapters, written or typed, of your completed manuscript to:

LDP: Submissions Dept
Po Box 870494
Mesquite, Tx 75187

DO NOT send original manuscript. Must be a duplicate.

Provide your synopsis and a cover letter containing your full contact information.

Thanks for considering LDP and Ca$h Presents.

BOW DOWN TO MY GANGSTA

By **Ca$h**

TORN BETWEEN TWO

By **Coffee**

BLOOD STAINS OF A SHOTTA **III**

By **Jamaica**

STEADY MOBBIN **III**

By **Marcellus Allen**

BLOOD OF A BOSS **VI**

SHADOWS OF THE GAME II

By **Askari**

LOYAL TO THE GAME **IV**

By **T.J. & Jelissa**

A DOPEBOY'S PRAYER **II**

By **Eddie "Wolf" Lee**

IF LOVING YOU IS WRONG… **III**

By **Jelissa**

TRUE SAVAGE **VII**

MIDNIGHT CARTEL

DOPE BOY MAGIC

By **Chris Green**

BLAST FOR ME **III**

DUFFLE BAG CARTEL **IV**

HEARTLESS GOON **III**

A SAVAGE DOPEBOY II

Drug Lords

DRUG LORDS II

By **Ghost**

A HUSTLER'S DECEIT III

KILL ZONE **II**

BAE BELONGS TO ME III

SOUL OF A MONSTER III

By **Aryanna**

THE COST OF LOYALTY **III**

By **Kweli**

THE SAVAGE LIFE III

By **J-Blunt**

KING OF NEW YORK V

COKE KINGS IV

BORN HEARTLESS III

By **T.J. Edwards**

GORILLAZ IN THE BAY V

De'Kari

THE STREETS ARE CALLING II

Duquie Wilson

KINGPIN KILLAZ IV

STREET KINGS III

PAID IN BLOOD III

CARTEL KILLAZ III

Hood Rich

SINS OF A HUSTLA II

ASAD

TRIGGADALE III

Elijah R. Freeman

KINGZ OF THE GAME V

Playa Ray

SLAUGHTER GANG IV

RUTHLESS HEART II

By Willie Slaughter

THE HEART OF A SAVAGE II

By Jibril Williams

FUK SHYT II

By Blakk Diamond

THE DOPEMAN'S BODYGAURD II

By Tranay Adams

TRAP GOD II

By Troublesome

YAYO II

A SHOOTER'S AMBITION II

By S. Allen

GHOST MOB

Stilloan Robinson

KINGPIN DREAMS

By Paper Boi Rari

CREAM

By Yolanda Moore

SON OF A DOPE FIEND II

By Renta

FOREVER GANGSTA II

By Adrian Dulan

LOYALTY AIN'T PROMISED

By Keith Williams

THE PRICE YOU PAY FOR LOVE

By Destiny Skai

THE LIFE OF A HOOD STAR

By Rashia Wilson

TOE TAGZ II

By Ah'Million

Available Now

RESTRAINING ORDER **I & II**

By **CA$H & Coffee**

LOVE KNOWS NO BOUNDARIES **I II & III**

By **Coffee**

RAISED AS A GOON I, II, III & IV

BRED BY THE SLUMS I, II, III

BLAST FOR ME I & II

ROTTEN TO THE CORE I II III

A BRONX TALE I, II, III

DUFFEL BAG CARTEL I II III

HEARTLESS GOON

A SAVAGE DOPEBOY

HEARTLESS GOON I II

DRUG LORDS

By **Ghost**

LAY IT DOWN **I & II**

Ghost

LAST OF A DYING BREED

BLOOD STAINS OF A SHOTTA I & II

By **Jamaica**

LOYAL TO THE GAME

LOYAL TO THE GAME II

LOYAL TO THE GAME III

LIFE OF SIN I, II III

By **TJ & Jelissa**

BLOODY COMMAS I & II

SKI MASK CARTEL I II & III

KING OF NEW YORK I II,III IV

RISE TO POWER I II III

COKE KINGS I II III

BORN HEARTLESS I II

By **T.J. Edwards**

IF LOVING HIM IS WRONG…I & II

LOVE ME EVEN WHEN IT HURTS I II III

By **Jelissa**

WHEN THE STREETS CLAP BACK I & II III

By **Jibril Williams**

A DISTINGUISHED THUG STOLE MY HEART I II & III

LOVE SHOULDN'T HURT I II III IV

RENEGADE BOYS I II III IV

By **Meesha**

A GANGSTER'S CODE I &, II III

A GANGSTER'S SYN I II III

THE SAVAGE LIFE I II

Drug Lords

By J-Blunt

PUSH IT TO THE LIMIT

By **Bre' Hayes**

BLOOD OF A BOSS **I, II, III, IV, V**

SHADOWS OF THE GAME

By **Askari**

THE STREETS BLEED MURDER **I, II & III**

THE HEART OF A GANGSTA I II& III

By **Jerry Jackson**

CUM FOR ME

CUM FOR ME 2

CUM FOR ME 3

CUM FOR ME 4

CUM FOR ME 5

An **LDP Erotica Collaboration**

BRIDE OF A HUSTLA **I II & II**

THE FETTI GIRLS **I, II& III**

CORRUPTED BY A GANGSTA I, II III, IV

BLINDED BY HIS LOVE

By **Destiny Skai**

WHEN A GOOD GIRL GOES BAD

By **Adrienne**

THE COST OF LOYALTY I II

By Kweli

A GANGSTER'S REVENGE **I II III & IV**

THE BOSS MAN'S DAUGHTERS

THE BOSS MAN'S DAUGHTERS II

Ghost

THE BOSSMAN'S DAUGHTERS III

THE BOSSMAN'S DAUGHTERS IV

THE BOSS MAN'S DAUGHTERS **V**

A SAVAGE LOVE **I & II**

BAE BELONGS TO ME I II

A HUSTLER'S DECEIT I, II, III

WHAT BAD BITCHES DO I, II, III

SOUL OF A MONSTER I II

KILL ZONE

By **Aryanna**

A KINGPIN'S AMBITON

A KINGPIN'S AMBITION **II**

I MURDER FOR THE DOUGH

By **Ambitious**

TRUE SAVAGE

TRUE SAVAGE II

TRUE SAVAGE **III**

TRUE SAVAGE **IV**

TRUE SAVAGE **V**

TRUE SAVAGE **VI**

By **Chris Green**

A DOPEBOY'S PRAYER

By **Eddie "Wolf" Lee**

THE KING CARTEL **I, II & III**

By **Frank Gresham**

THESE NIGGAS AIN'T LOYAL **I, II & III**

By **Nikki Tee**

Drug Lords

GANGSTA SHYT **I II &III**

By **CATO**

THE ULTIMATE BETRAYAL

By **Phoenix**

BOSS'N UP **I , II & III**

By **Royal Nicole**

I LOVE YOU TO DEATH

By Destiny J

I RIDE FOR MY HITTA

I STILL RIDE FOR MY HITTA

By **Misty Holt**

LOVE & CHASIN' PAPER

By **Qay Crockett**

TO DIE IN VAIN

SINS OF A HUSTLA

By **ASAD**

BROOKLYN HUSTLAZ

By **Boogsy Morina**

BROOKLYN ON LOCK I & II

By **Sonovia**

GANGSTA CITY

By **Teddy Duke**

A DRUG KING AND HIS DIAMOND I & II III

A DOPEMAN'S RICHES

HER MAN, MINE'S TOO I, II

CASH MONEY HO'S

By Nicole Goosby

Ghost

TRAPHOUSE KING **I II & III**

KINGPIN KILLAZ I II III

STREET KINGS I II

PAID IN BLOOD **I II**

CARTEL KILLAZ I II

By **Hood Rich**

LIPSTICK KILLAH **I, II, III**

CRIME OF PASSION I II & III

By **Mimi**

STEADY MOBBN' **I, II, III**

By **Marcellus Allen**

WHO SHOT YA **I, II, III**

SON OF A DOPE FIEND

Renta

GORILLAZ IN THE BAY **I II III IV**

DE'KARI

TRIGGADALE I II

Elijah R. Freeman

GOD BLESS THE TRAPPERS I, II, III

THESE SCANDALOUS STREETS I, II, III

FEAR MY GANGSTA I, II, III

THESE STREETS DON'T LOVE NOBODY I, II

BURY ME A G I, II, III, IV, V

A GANGSTA'S EMPIRE I, II, III, IV

THE DOPEMAN'S BODYGAURD

Tranay Adams

THE STREETS ARE CALLING

Drug Lords

Duquie Wilson

MARRIED TO A BOSS... I II III

By Destiny Skai & Chris Green

KINGZ OF THE GAME I II III IV

Playa Ray

SLAUGHTER GANG I II III

RUTHLESS HEART

By Willie Slaughter

THE HEART OF A SAVAGE

By Jibril Williams

FUK SHYT

By Blakk Diamond

DON'T F#CK WITH MY HEART I II

By Linnea

ADDICTED TO THE DRAMA I II III

By Jamila

YAYO

A SHOOTER'S AMBITION

By S. Allen

TRAP GOD

By Troublesome

FOREVER GANGSTA

By Adrian Dulan

TOE TAGZ

By Ah'Million

BOOKS BY LDP'S CEO, CA$H

TRUST IN NO MAN

TRUST IN NO MAN 2

TRUST IN NO MAN 3

BONDED BY BLOOD

SHORTY GOT A THUG

THUGS CRY

THUGS CRY 2

THUGS CRY 3

TRUST NO BITCH

TRUST NO BITCH 2

TRUST NO BITCH 3

TIL MY CASKET DROPS

RESTRAINING ORDER

RESTRAINING ORDER 2

IN LOVE WITH A CONVICT

Coming Soon

BONDED BY BLOOD 2

BOW DOWN TO MY GANGSTA

Drug Lords